MW01277910

HUNT TO KILL

REED MONTGOMERY BOOK 2

LOGAN RYLES

Paperback ISBN: 978-1-7323819-6-4

Hardcover ISBN: 979-8-7679544-5-2

Library of Congress Control Number: 2019913233

Published by Ryker Morgan Publishing.

Cover design by Rafido Designs.

ALSO BY LOGAN RYLES

The Reed Montgomery Series

Prequel: *Sandbox*, a short story (read for free at LoganRyles.com)

Book 1: *Overwatch*

Book 2: *Hunt to Kill*

Book 3: *Total War*

Book 4: *Smoke and Mirrors*

Book 5: *Survivor*

Book 6: *Death Cycle*

Book 7: *Sundown*

The Prosecution Force Series

Book 1: *Brink of War*

The Wolfgang Pierce Series

Prequel: *That Time in Appalachia* (read for free at LoganRyles.com)

Book 1: *That Time in Paris*

Book 2: *That Time in Cairo*

For 2LT I.R.K., Alabama Army National Guard.

My original fan.

1

November 24, 2014
United States Military Court
Washington, DC

"Reed Montgomery, on the charge of conduct unbecoming a United States Marine, you have been found *guilty*. On the charge of five counts of first-degree murder, you have been found *guilty*. You are hereby stripped of your rank and dishonorably discharged from the United States Armed Forces."

The judge paused over the conviction papers, his weary shoulders dropping a little but his tone remaining resolute.

"The murder of Private Jeanie O'Conner was a deplorable act. But I nevertheless find your deliberate execution of five US citizens to be a crime of the worst character, and I am unconvinced of any remorse on your part. I am therefore compelled to sentence you to death. Sergeant, take the guilty into custody!"

The gavel rang like a gunshot. The sharp *shrick* of the corporal patches being torn from Reed's sleeves filled his ears, screaming over the pounding of blood. Cold cuffs closed around his wrists, and the tall military policeman wearing sergeant's patches grabbed him by the arm and shoved him toward the door. Boots clicked on the tile, and the air was thick and hot, like the oppressive nights of Baghdad.

Private Rufus "Turk" Turkman, Reed's long-time brother-in-arms, stood next to the door. Reed met his gaze and mouthed a single word: "Goodbye."

"Next!" The stocky sergeant behind the desk bellowed at the line of white-clad prisoners without looking up. His face was pale and blotchy, betraying a life spent sitting behind that desk, away from the sun, and barking at convicts.

Reed shuffled forward, twisting his wrists against the tight cuffs. His footfalls rang against the blank block walls, leaving dark black scuffs on the dirty concrete. In the corner, a desk heater's electric coils glowed red in a futile attempt to provide warmth to the uninsulated space.

"Name," the sergeant demanded.

"Montgomery. Reed."

A pen scratched on yellow paper. The metal table squeaked under the pressure, and Reed swallowed back the knots in his stomach. He twisted his wrists again and tried to keep from shivering.

God, it's cold. The whole place can't be this cold.

"All right." The sergeant spoke without looking up. "Listen carefully, and don't speak until I'm finished. You are a prisoner of the United States Armed Forces. While renovations are completed at Fort Leavenworth, you will be housed at this facility. As such, you are our guest and will behave accordingly at all times. Is that clear?"

"Yes."

"Excellent. This institution is the property and function of the state of Colorado, and you can expect it to be operated according to our laws. Colorado does not automatically isolate death row inmates such as yourself. You will be confined in gen pop with other max security prisoners. This housing arrangement is a *privilege*, and can and will be revoked at any time should you become insubordinate. Do you understand?"

"I do."

"Good. You will abide by all daily functions, including lights out, waking hours, housekeeping duties, and any commands given to you by correctional officers. Any insurrection, insubordination, contraband, violence, or disruptive behavior will be swiftly and severely punished. Is that clear?"

"Yes."

The sergeant laid down the pen, and for the first time, he faced Reed. "You carry a death sentence. Men such as yourself often find themselves feeling desperate. Listen to me carefully when I tell you we do not tolerate desperate behavior. No matter who you are or where you came from, I promise you, you *do not* want to test us. This isn't a white-collar resort with a chain-link fence. We have the power to make your life absolute hell. Do you understand me?"

The heater hummed in the corner, providing the only variance to the silence. Those wide, bloodshot eyes didn't blink, and neither did Reed's. Seconds dripped by as though they were falling from a slow-leaking faucet.

"So, you're one of those." The sergeant nodded and tapped his pen against the table. "We'll see how long that lasts. Officer Yates! Show the convict to his cell."

An iron grip latched around Reed's arm, and he was propelled out of the room through a back door and into a long hallway. The CO's boots clicked amid the shuffle of the ankle chains, and with each step, Reed's chest constricted a little tighter. Dim lights shone down over him, barely illuminating the black dirt packed into the floor's cracks or the scratches in the paint along the walls. Dingy yellow ceiling panels hung overhead, completing the mood of the most utilitarian, unwelcoming place Reed could imagine.

"Move it, con." The correctional officer snapped and pushed harder. The chains caught on his ankles, and Reed stumbled around the corner. Two more halls, one flight of steps, and then a tall metal door with no window. Voices and footsteps rang out on the other side, pounding through a cavernous room beyond. Reed tripped over the threshold and fell to his knees, crashing against concrete. White pants flashing back and forth across the floor filled his vision.

A hundred yards ahead of him, standing in neat two-story rows, were dozens of small cells. Steel bars with open sliding doors guarded them, and a hundred white-clothed convicts wandered around the floor. Fluorescent light glowed from someplace far above, joined by a single bar-covered window at the top of the wall. The floor was as hard as the block hallways behind him, and there was no other way out. No doors. No color. No warmth. Only cold, brutal containment.

The CO grabbed him by the arm and hauled him to his feet. His fingers dug into Reed's arm, sending waves of pain shooting up to his shoulder. He fought to find his footing as he was shoved forward.

"Welcome to Rock Hollow Penitentiary, Number 4371."

"What's your name?"

Reed sat on the edge of the bed, his feet resting on the cell's chilled floor. He rubbed his bare wrists, massaging the bruises left by the cuffs. The thin white coverall suit he wore was incapable of blocking the bite of impending winter. Nothing could stop that scourge.

"Hey. You deaf?"

Reed looked up. A tall, skinny man with a shiny bald head and no hair on his pale face stood in the doorway to the cell, one hand resting on the wall, the other jammed in his pocket. His eyes were grey and hollow, like twin black holes frozen over.

"I'm Reed." The words left his lips as a dry monotone. He swallowed and tried to clear his throat.

The tall man nodded, still expressionless. "Is that right? Well, what the hell are you doing on my bed, Reed?"

Reed placed his hands on the thin blanket stretched over the cheap mattress. The stiff plastic sheathing crackled under his touch. He stood up and stepped away, offering a small shrug. "I'll take the top."

Reed placed his palms on the top bunk, preparing to lift himself onto the mattress, when cold fingers wrapped around his wrist, tightening into his skin.

The tall man leaned in close, his breath, reeking of garlic and cheap food, misting just inches from Reed's face. "That's my bed, too."

The comment felt distantly preposterous to Reed, as though he should laugh. But through the fog of disorientation, he couldn't make sense of it. He tilted his head and stepped back, gesturing toward the small cell. "Where the hell do I sleep?"

The man laughed, then jerked a thumb toward the stainless steel toilet mounted against the wall. "Sitting up. Like the bitch you are."

Reed stared at the toilet. The comments didn't register. Was this a joke? Was this man insane?

"Hey! What'd I tell you about coming in here? Get your skinny ass back into the hall!"

A snapping, high-pitched voice filled the cell, coming from behind the tall man. Reed started and stepped back as a short guy with dark hair barreled through the door. He wore the same white coveralls, but they fell low around his ankles and almost covered his hands. He couldn't have been more than five and a half feet tall, but his shoulders bulged, and even through the loose outfit, Reed could see the power of his muscled core.

The short man grabbed the tall one by the back of his coveralls and shoved him toward the door with another curse. "Go back to your hole, creep! I catch you slinking around here again, and you'll catch a shiv in the ribs. You hear me?"

The tall man cast one more sinister look toward Reed, then vanished down the hallway. The sound of barking voices from the crowd of convicts drowned out his footfalls. Reed leaned against the wall, feeling all the more disoriented.

The short man ran his fingers through dark curls, still glowering at the door. Then he shot a semi-interested glance at Reed. "You must be the fresh meat. Welcome to the pen." He extended his fist, then waited for Reed to bump it. His knuckles were hard with thick callouses built over them. He nodded at Reed once, then turned toward the bed and began to stretch the wrinkles out of the blanket. "I'm Stiller. You can call me *Still* if you want. I'm your celly. You want top or bottom?"

Reed placed his hand on the rail of the top bunk and ran his finger against the smooth surface. Flecks of ancient lead paint and grime rained onto the floor, and the stench of unwashed bodies and years of sweat filled his nostrils. The edge of the rail dug into his finger, and he dropped his hand back to his side.

I've slept on concrete that was more welcoming.

Stiller waited, then chuckled. "The fresh meat daze! Still can't believe it's real, huh? Well, take it from me, homie. It's real. Sooner you own it, the better your life will be. You take the bottom bunk. I won't sleep well with a dude your size hanging over me."

Stiller kicked off his shoes before hoisting himself onto the upper bunk. "You got a name or what?"

"Reed. Reed Montgomery."

"A pleasure, Reed. What'd you do?"

Reed folded his arms and leaned against the wall. The concrete bit into his shoulder blades, but he didn't move. He clenched his fists into his armpits and closed his eyes.

Stiller laughed again. "So, you're one of those. Whatever makes you feel better. Myself, I got busted dealing dope. I got a dime, still eight to go."

Reed pushed his hands into his pockets, searching for warmth to thaw his numb fingers.

"At least tell me how long you're in for," Stiller said.

Reed hesitated, then slumped over. It didn't really matter, he guessed. "Until they finish renovations at Leavenworth. I'll be there until . . . it's over."

Stiller frowned, tilting his head, and then an apparent realization dawned on him. He sighed. "Damn sorry to hear that, Reed. May you find favor with the appeals gods."

Reed shrugged and looked out into the hallway. "Who was he? The tall guy."

Stiller grunted. "They call him *Milk*. No idea what his real name is. Even the COs call him that."

"Is he dangerous?"

Stiller chuckled again. The sound was strangely comforting.

"Dude, you need to understand something. *Everyone* in here is dangerous. Milk isn't particularly burly, but he's shady and ruthless, and he's got a lot of friends. A lot of bitches, too—people who fear him and run his errands. My guess is, he was here to test the waters with you."

Reed stared into the hallway, rubbing his fingers together inside the pockets. They were still numb, but a hint of warmth built between the folds of the fabric.

"Did he try to push you around? Demean you?" Stiller said. Reed grunted, and Stiller leaned back into the pillow. "Yep. He's testing you. Better deal with it, Reed. It's not something you wanna leave hanging."

Reed kicked off his shoes and sat on the edge of the bed, looking at the blank, merciless floor between his feet. "I'm not here to fight. I just wanna—"

"Do your time and be left alone." Stiller finished the sentence with another snort. He rolled over on the bunk, and then his head appeared upside down next to Reed's. He had a handsome face with two days' worth of scruff on his cheeks. "Let me give you some advice, Reed. Best case scenario, you get off death row and spend the rest of your life inside a cell. Worst case scenario, you work through the appeals courts for the next ten years, and they still kill you. Either way, you're gonna be in prison for a hot minute. It's up to you how hot that minute is." Stiller slid off the bunk and shoved his feet back into the shoes, then shuffled through the open door.

Metal and shoes rattled outside the cell, and the grey walls around Reed blurred out of focus. Everything closed around him, drawing in toward his skull. Reed staggered to the sink and splashed water on his face, gasping for air as he clutched the edges of the basin. His reflection in the dirty mirror showed the white pallor of his cheeks and the panic in his eyes.

I can't stay here.

2

Rock Hollow Penitentiary

"Lights! Lights!"

The sharp *pop, pop* of the industrial switches preceded a flood of light blazing into the cell. Reed blinked and groaned, pulling the blanket over his face.

Stiller crashed to the floor beside him, then smacked him on the arm. "Get up, Reed. It's not an option."

More clanging resounded outside, this time on the second level, and growing closer. Reed pushed his feet out of bed and dropped to the floor. The shoes were tight around his toes, and a new shiver ripped through his body as he shuffled toward the locked door.

Two grey-clad correctional officers stomped in front of his cell, and a metal flashlight clicked against the bars before blasting his face with light. The beam swept over both bunks before the guards disappeared toward the next cell.

"They'll open the doors and order us out. Fall in behind me. Keep your hands out of your pockets, and walk with the others. Don't talk to the guards."

Reed reluctantly pulled his hands from his pockets and shifted on the hard floor.

What time is it? How long did I sleep?

There was no time in this place. No concept of day or night. It could've been three in the afternoon for all he knew.

"Open full block!" The command snapped from the end of the hallway, and the electric controls of the doors squeaked and groaned. Each steel door slid open.

"All convicts, *fall in*!" The voice boomed over the speakers, buried out of sight in the ceiling high above. Stiller stepped out of the cell and turned left. Reed followed him and stood behind, looking down the long line of white-clad prisoners. Nobody spoke. All eyes were directed at the line of COs standing on the ground level, brooding and swinging nightsticks on the ends of leather lanyards.

"*Move out!*"

Jumpsuit legs swished against one another, releasing body odor down the hallway as the column of convicts migrated toward the door. The lights flickered, and sweat filled Reed's palms as he clenched them against his sides.

Someone shoved him in the lower back, and Reed looked over his shoulder.

A tall, cross-eyed man gave him a crooked grin. One eye stared at Reed while the other twitched at random. "Fresh meat," he hissed.

Reed shot him an icy glare and faced forward again. Doors and hallways flashed past—one flight of stairs, then two metal gates that opened into a wide courtyard outside. Block walls topped with razor wire surrounded them, canopied by a black sky without a hint of sun. White spotlights drove the shadows into the far corners of the yard.

"Line up on the grid," Stiller whispered.

Reed followed him down the sidewalk and stopped on a wide white line. The other prisoners followed suit, forming into eight neat rows of twenty men standing shoulder to shoulder. The air was bitter cold, biting straight through the thin coveralls and into Reed's bones, making every joint feel stiff and brittle.

"*Count off!*" the lead CO shouted from the end of the first line.

His cohorts walked between the lines of prisoners, tapping each one on the arm as they counted. Reed stiffened as a nightstick smacked against his elbow, and the CO passed without making eye contact.

The private from the end of the line called back to the sergeant at the front of the courtyard. "All prisoners present and accounted for, sir!"

"You may begin the drill, Officer."

Reed's stomach fluttered, and he looked at Stiller. "Drill?"

Stiller squeezed his eyes shut. "Contraband. They found contraband. This is what happens."

"All right, you cons. On the ground!"

The men around him fell on their stomachs. Reed followed, placing his hands beneath his chest as the private began to count off. One, two. Each pushup burned, sending prickling heat shooting down the backs of his arms. Within minutes, a pool of sweat built on the concrete under his nose. Stiller pumped up and down beside him without a sound, his face down, vision fixed on the pavement.

Reed gritted his teeth and continued as the CO at the end of the line shouted the count. They passed the thirty mark and kept going. The ache building in his back ran toward his tailbone, but Reed's hardened muscles tightened and delivered.

"On your feet! *Move it!*"

All one hundred sixty men scrambled up, and a clapping resounded from the nearest CO.

He jerked his arm toward the nearest block wall. "*Laps!* Let's go!"

The crowd of sweaty men piled in along the walls and began to circle the courtyard, running as the CO continued to shout commands and urge them onward. Reed had run many times in his life. It was his favorite exercise during boot camp—simple, rhythmic, and predictable—but this was totally different. Men slammed into his back and shoved him sideways, making it almost impossible to maintain his pace. The crush of bodies around him was like a swarm of fish, all piled on top of each other and desperately trying to escape the wide, open mouth of a killer whale.

"*Faster! Let's go!*"

Reed gasped for breath and pushed back the mental revulsion to the burn in his legs. The world spun around him, still covered by a black sky. One lap followed another, broken into segments of a hundred yards by fifty yards. Some of the men flagged and stumbled, but were driven on by shouting COs.

"Halt!"

The long column fell over each other as they collapsed against the fences and the ground. Reed held his stomach and gasped. A tinge of orange slowly brightened the sky over the mountains.

"Fall in! Showers!"

The column of prisoners slipped through the gates and back into the hallways, working their way up two flights of steps. The prison was alive now with blazing lights and the clamor of guards and workers. As they passed one of the dining rooms, the sour stench of stale grease took away any appetite Reed might have had. Everything was old, dingy, and utilitarian. No hint of beauty or life touched this place. It was like a graveyard for the living.

One more hallway opened into a wide room with tile floors and rows of showerheads on the walls. There were no partitions, and a draft blew in from someplace overhead.

"Strip! Let's go!"

The prisoners shucked their sweat-soaked coveralls and dumped them into a line of laundry carts. As Reed peeled off the sticky garment, he searched for Stiller, but his undersized cellmate had already disappeared somewhere in the line of naked bodies that formed between the carts and the showerheads. Reed stepped back to the end of the line and held his hands loosely at his sides, flexing his toes over the cold tiles.

Where the hell am I?

He joined the Marines to get out. Get out of Southern California, out of the gangs, out of his mother's boyfriend's stinking apartment. To be free. Be on his own. How had that vanished so quickly?

Nothing was what he expected. Not that he gave a lot of thought to what prison would be like. He assumed it would entail long periods of downtime, sitting in a cell by himself, staring at a wall. Forced PT, mass showers, and screaming COs hadn't entered into that equation.

He thought back over the past year, back before the courtrooms, the trial, and the handcuffs. Back to Iraq. Back to the sand and the heat and the bullets. And O'Conner. He saw her lying dead in the dirt with a bloodied face and the haunted, empty eyes of a woman who hours before had held enough spirit to tame a dragon. Now gone. Crushed like a roach against hardwood.

The hard edge of a nightstick smacked Reed on the arm, and a CO glowered at him. "Move it, con! Let's go!"

Reed hurried to close the gap between himself and the end of the line. As the room began to empty, a shower became available. The water that streamed over his back was lukewarm at best, but still eased the tension in his taut muscles. Flakes of greasy soap broke off the bar as Reed rubbed it against his armpits. He tried not to think about how many dozens of smelly bodies had collided with that bar since it assumed residency at the top of a mildew-encrusted ledge next to the showerhead. Somehow, soap still felt more sanitary than water alone, no matter how greasy. He spat a stream of over-chlorinated water against the wall and replaced the soap on the ledge.

I'd do it again.

The thought rang as clearly in his head as it had the past July, right before he chambered a round into his rifle and aligned the scope with the base of Commander Gould's neck. He pulled that trigger because he had no choice. Something snapped inside of him when he first saw Private O'Conner's brutalized corpse. From that moment, everything that happened was automated.

Inevitable.

And now this.

"Well, well . . . Looks like it's just you and me again, bitch."

Reed blinked away the soap and water. The voice was familiar, smooth, and venomous.

Milk stood five feet away, his wet hair dripping over a naked, bony frame. One hand draped over his exposed crotch, slowly rubbing back and forth, while his eyes blazed at Reed over a twisted smile. "You *are* a bitch, aren't you? You look like a bitch. A lot like the bitch I took back in Nebraska. Oh, but she wasn't as smart as you. She screamed bloody murder like she wasn't even enjoying it. You're smarter, aren't you? You know what's good for you."

Reed cast a quick glance around the shower room. The COs were gone, as were the remainder of the prisoners—all except two tall, beefy men with thick arms that swung next to bulging guts as they closed in a few steps behind Milk. Reed recognized one of the goons by his cross-eyed glare, one eye fixed on his prey while the other roamed the room at random. Their bare feet smacked against the tile as water droplets cascaded over still-dirty hair.

Milk took a step forward, running a skinny tongue over his lips. "All right, then. Make it quick and strong if you know what's good for you." He took another step and touched Reed's arm.

Reed slid to the right before grabbing Milk by the throat and placing his other hand against the base of the man's skull. A lightning twist of his torso propelled Milk's face directly into the wall. Flesh met tile with a crack, and blood exploded over Reed's hands. He stepped back and grabbed Milk by the shoulder, then swept his left foot across the floor and into Milk's shins at the same moment he pushed down on the shoulder. The creep crashed to the floor with a scream.

Before Reed could turn, Milk's goons were on top of him, throwing him into the wall a millisecond before one of their meaty fists slammed home into his gut. He clutched his stomach as another fist caught him in the chin, followed by a knee to the groin.

An eruption of pain flooded through him, weakening all other sensations as Reed flailed out with both arms. Another blow to his stomach and his vision began to tunnel. Thick fingers closed around his throat, choking out the air and forcing his head into the tile.

"Night-night, bitch," the voice rumbled, half-chuckle, half-snarl.

No. Not this way.

Reed launched his fist forward in one more blind attempt to dislodge the grip on his throat, and he felt the satisfying crack of a nose collapsing beneath his knuckles. The fingers fell off his throat, and he gasped for air. Then a fist flashed into Reed's view just as it tore through the air and crashed into his head.

3

Lights from overhead burned through Reed's eyelids. His clouded eyes felt both crusty and moist, blurring out the big, blotchy face that leaned over his. A medical mask was stretched over the nose, just below dark eyes. Reed tried twisting to get a better view, but his body was restrained by some thick strap circumventing his stomach. The familiar bite of handcuffs on either wrist secured his arms to the table.

The distinct sting of a needle pierced his face once, then twice. With each push of the needle, fingers twitched against his skin, stitching one thread after another into his cheek. The pain restored his memory, and he saw Milk's sneering face leaning over him again. The anger returned, along with maddening frustration.

"Is he conscious?"

The man in the mask grunted, and a new face appeared beside his. It was the desk sergeant who checked Reed into the prison on his first day.

"I knew you'd be trouble, Montgomery." There was no hint of sympathy in the cold voice.

Reed grunted and tried to twist again, then remembered the restraints. "They jumped me."

"Is that right? By the look of it, you were happy to join in on the fun."

There was nothing Reed could say. The sergeant would either believe him or he wouldn't. Either way, not much was likely to change.

The sergeant barked at the medical officer. "What's his prognosis?"

The man in the mask grunted again, then snipped the end of the thread with a pair of scissors. "Cuts and bruises. He'll be fine."

"Very good." The sergeant snapped his fingers. "Officer!"

The door opened, and another CO stepped in.

"Take 4371 to isolation. Book him for three weeks. Minimum rations."

The private slid the handcuffs and belt off of Reed. As he stood, head spinning, the private closed his hard fingers around his arm.

"Learn your lesson, Montgomery." The sergeant's voice was unsympathetic. "There's no forgiveness here."

The CO shoved him forward through the door and into a hall.

Another oversized pair of white coveralls swished against his legs with each step, but his feet were bare. Bruises and aching joints fogged his mind, making each step agony. His head ached harder than ever, and his tongue stuck to the roof of a dry mouth.

Light flooded his eyes as the private pushed him out into another courtyard. This one was much larger than the first, with grass and park benches. Small crowds of convicts stood around the perimeter, talking or milling about. Sneers and smirks, mixed with a handful of blank stares, met Reed's gaze. The CO pushed him along the sidewalk, down the fence line, and toward the isolation ward. As Reed stumbled on he noticed a scrawny man bent over a park bench with his back turned. Two other men stood nearby with their arms folded across their chests. Reed squinted against the bright sunlight, watching as Milk turned toward him, his face wrapped in a thick bandage.

Reed jerked free of the guard and made a dash toward the table before the nightstick descended over the back of his head. A light crack, just sharp enough to send disorientation and nausea washing through his body.

He shoved the guard back and stumbled toward Milk, wrapping his fingers into a tight fist. "I'll rip your throat out!"

Another blow from the nightstick crashed into his arm. Fingers dug into the collar of his jumpsuit, pulling him off balance as more COs rushed in to subdue him.

Reed kicked out with both feet, swinging his elbow backward until it connected with somebody's chin. "Let me at him! He started it, dammit!"

"Shut up, con!"

Two more COs piled on top of him, and Reed jerked free of the first, launching himself out of the pile and back onto his feet. Milk stood ten feet away, his eyes alight with devilish glee as he twisted his head backward and stuck his tongue out as though he were strangling at the end of a noose.

The guards grabbed Reed, overpowering him and dragging him backward. He gave up the fight, but found Milk's eyes one last time and mouthed a warning: "*I'm coming for you.*"

"Don't do it, Reed. Whatever happened. Whatever you know. You can't come back from this."

Grey mist swarmed and danced around Turk's face. His words were distant, as though they were coming from the other side of a cavern—echoing, but familiar. Reed touched Turk's shoulder and imagined the rough, dirty texture of the military jacket, but it felt thin and wispy, as though Turk were a ghost. But it wasn't a ghost. He knew this marine. Turk was his best friend and the last surviving member of his fire team back in Iraq. His right-hand man.

"Neither can she." Reed's own words echoed through the mist and darkness, and his body felt detached from his voice.

The words tasted bitter. God, why are they so bitter? They flew from his mouth like venom. Reed shoved past Turk as fireworks burst, lighting up his path as he weaved between the barracks. Dry sand crunched beneath his feet. The rifle was heavy, but with each stride, fresh confidence—and fresh anger—flooded his body.

Where am I? Why is it all so familiar? And so distant?

Men in black with beer bottles and cigarettes were gathered around a table—smoking, drinking, laughing. One of them leaned over the table, pumping his hips into its edge, dramatizing the motion while the others laughed. These weren't marines. No, they were contractors. Mercenaries.

"Give it to her! Smack that bitch!" The shout was slurred, laden with alcohol.

Five of them. Reed squinted into the scope of the rifle, aligning the crosshairs with the base of the first man's neck.

Commander Gould. The prick.

That first gunshot shattered their laughter but was lost amongst the blast of Independence Day fireworks overhead. Gould went down, blood gushing from his stomach over the Iraqi dust. Reed stepped ahead and fired again. There were shouts, and then a handgun popped. Something ripped into his shoulder.

The thunk of the bolt locking back over an empty magazine resonated through Reed's arm. Through the blur of rage and adrenaline, he saw four bodies lying in the swirling mist with gaping mouths and pale cheeks. The fifth man lay on his side with blood gushing from his hip as he clawed at the sand, pulling himself away from the corpses of his comrades.

Reed knew his face—a strong brow line, low cheekbones, a bold chin. Even in the darkness that hung around him, he recognized Commander Gould's defiant glare.

The shriek of metal against metal rang through the stillness as Reed's knife cleared its sheath. Someplace on the other side of the fog, men shouted. There were gunshots, too —short and popping, the familiar voice of a handgun. A bullet hissed past Reed's ear as he stepped over the last body and placed his muddy boot against Gould's shoulder, pinning him into the dirt.

"Remember me, Gould?"

The commander's face twisted into a smile, then his features morphed as his teeth became fangs and his hair horns. It was no longer the face of a civilian contractor. It was the face of a demon, snarling back at him in blatant defiance.

Reed plunged the knife into the demon's throat. The gunshots roared behind him now, and bullets tore through his back, blasting holes in his chest that gleamed like stars as he jerked the knife free and plunged it home again. The blood that gushed free of the demon's throat wasn't red—it was inky black. Thick and hot.

Reed sat up with a scream. Cold sweat ran down his face as he fumbled through the darkness. The tiny isolation cell was complete and consuming. He grabbed to his right and felt the block wall. As his feet hit the floor, he focused on the opposing wall, only four feet separated from its twin.

He dug his fingers into the mattress, holding on as he imagined the walls closing in around him.

No. I can't do it. I can't do it.

Reed stood up and slung himself against the steel door, driving his fist into it. The tiny cell rang with the clatter, and he screamed for the guard. No lights flooded on, and no boots rang against the hallways. Only silence answered his desperate outburst.

The mattress squeaked as he collapsed back against it, and at once, the visions returned. Blood. Carnage. Bodies everywhere. Eyes open or closed, he could still see their faces—the haunted stares of the slain. He didn't feel regret, and no hint of remorse haunted his soul, but he felt the burning desire to destroy the last remaining traces of the ghosts from Iraq.

Reed clamped his eyes shut in an attempt to extinguish the flames dancing behind his eyelids. But even here, in the darkness and silence, there was no peace—only anger and the crushing reality that his life was a joke. Maybe it always had been. His earliest memories weren't like this. They were happy. His father was a free man and a successful finance professional. His mother was a local environmental activist, and she was sober, still something of a basket case on her worst days, but nothing like the slobbering, skanky drunk she became after her husband was hauled off to federal prison for money laundering.

Reed tried to calm his nerves by remembering those days when his family was a family. They lived in Mountain Brook, Alabama, an upscale suburb of Birmingham. Tabitha Montgomery used to make Toaster Strudels in the morning before Reed got on the bus, and ham and potatoes on Sundays for lunch. She always fussed about feeding him sugar first thing in the morning, but Dave Montgomery came to his son's rescue. Dave was like that. Fun and happy. He told cheesy jokes and was friends with all the neighbors—the kind of guy you might ask to borrow a hand tool from and wind up sitting on the back patio sipping beer and swapping war stories with. Everybody loved him.

Maybe that was why she left, Reed thought.

Maybe that was why, after her husband's conviction and sentencing, Tabitha couldn't stay in her beloved hometown anymore. Too many people knew her, knew Dave, and knew little Reed. There were too many patronizing stares at the grocery store, too many whispering gossips at the local Baptist church. It was a level of shame and displacement she couldn't handle, so she did the next logical thing: pack up her son and what was left of her belongings after the federal confiscations, and move as far away as she could.

Reed opened his eyes and stared at the dark ceiling. He imagined his mother's face: the bags under her bloodshot eyes, another glass of vodka held between thin, greasy fingers. Los Angeles hadn't been kind to her, just like it hadn't been kind to him. At eighteen, Reed was only weeks away from being accepted into a south LA gang when the Marine recruiter confronted him outside a restaurant.

The sergeant wore green camouflage and a glare that could melt stone, but when he looked at Reed, he smiled. "You're about to screw up your whole life, kid. What a shame. A guy like you could make a hell of a Marine. Guess the apple doesn't fall far from the tree, huh?"

Reed rubbed his finger against the steel rail of his bunk and closed his eyes again. He never asked the recruiter how he knew about his father. He never asked him what the pay was or what career opportunities he would have in the Corps. He didn't even ask where they would send him. He just walked after him, caught the recruiter by the sleeve, and said, "You're wrong. Where do I sign?"

The edge of the bedrail sliced into Reed's thumb, and he snatched his hand back. The tiny cell closed in on him again, and he sucked in a humid breath.

All that sacrifice. All that war. And they threw me in here without a second thought.

He pressed his thumb against the dirty sheets until the bleeding subsided. He couldn't see Tabitha's face anymore. He couldn't hear the Marine recruiter challenging him with that gruff, disgusted voice. All he could hear was a single thought, pounding through his skull as loud and insistent as a war chant.

I have to get out of here.

———

4

The dining hall clattered as plastic plates were set onto steel dining tables. Reed rubbed his wrists.

The CO standing at his side raised an eyebrow then jerked his head toward the mess line twenty feet away. "Get to it, 4371. No talking."

Reed stepped into the back of the line and waited his turn to fill his plate. The dining hall rang with the clinking of utensils and the murmur of voices. COs stood in the corners, their narrow eyes surveying the crowd of convicts. A few of the prisoners looked at Reed with detached curiosity, but nobody spoke to him.

A cafeteria worker slopped runny mashed potatoes piled high next to dry ham and a wilting salad onto Reed's plate. He remembered eating with Turk in Baghdad at the military mess halls. That food was a feast compared to the stale slop on his plate now.

He took a seat at a table near the back of the room and ate quietly, searching the room for any sign of Milk or his comrades. A few faces were familiar, and the others were men with big shoulders and stern glares, tattoos adorning their skin, exposed by rolled-up sleeves. Nobody smiled. Nobody laughed.

Ignoring the slimy texture of the salad and dressing, Reed shoveled more food into his mouth. At least he could see what he was eating. That was an improvement over the lightless dungeon of solitary confinement.

The door at the far end of the room opened, and a CO stepped out first, followed by a small crowd of prisoners. Reed immediately spotted Milk standing at the back, a surly smirk playing at the corners of his mouth. When he saw Reed, his smile widened and his eyes flashed as before, but he turned away and shuffled toward the meal line. Reed watched him over the top rim of his water cup, taking slow sips and muting out the chaos around him. Only the pale man in coveralls mattered.

"He's not worth it. Trust me."

Reed recoiled, clenching his fist and raising it to defend himself. A short white man in a prison jumpsuit stood behind him, his stubby arms jammed into his pockets. He squinted at Reed, and without breaking eye contact, tilted his head toward a nearby CO.

Reed traced his gaze to the correctional officer, then lowered his fist.

The short man shuffled forward and sat down on the bench across from him, his hands still in his pockets. "You're quite the fighter, in spite of your total lack of discretion. That's why you're here, isn't it?"

"Who the hell are you?" Reed spat the words, surprised by his own aggression.

"I don't know, 4371. *Who are you*?"

Reed scoffed and stuck his fork into the last clump of cold potatoes. "Get lost."

Silence hung between them for a moment, but the little man didn't move.

When Reed looked up again, the narrow black eyes were still locked on him, and his fork rang against the plate. "I said, beat it!"

The short man withdrew his hands from his pockets and placed them on the table. One finger was missing from his right hand, and his other fingers were short and stumpy like the rest of his body.

"Think very carefully about what you're about to do," he said. "I know you can kill him. *You* know you can kill him. He probably knows it, too. But you'll be caught. And when you are, there'll be zero chance of your death penalty being lifted."

Reed's fork hung in midair, a piece of leathery ham stuck to the end. "How do you know about that?"

"I know a lot of things, Reed. A lot of things you'd like to know."

Once more, Reed let the silence hang in the air between them as he waited for the man to either blink or look away. He did neither.

"All right," Reed said. "I'll bite. What do you know?"

The little man drummed his fingers on the table, then smiled. "I know how to get you out of here."

Reed snorted. "Let me guess. Through the door?"

"It's not a joke, Reed. I know how to get you out."

This time the silence was palpable, like the emptiness of a tomb. Reed stopped chewing, once more trying to force the man to blink, but he wouldn't. His gaze was as unbroken and relentless as the block walls that encased them.

"Who are you?" Reed demanded.

"Call me Gould."

Reed slammed the fork against the plate, wiped his mouth on his sleeve, then clenched his fist over the tabletop. "Okay. So you know all about me. What do you want?"

"I want you to do what you do best. I want you to kill somebody. Somebody in this prison. Except this time, I want you to get away with it."

"And why the hell would I do that?"

"Because after you do, you'll walk out a free man. No death penalty. No FBI hounds on your heels. No criminal record to hide from. A fresh start."

"You know something, *Gould*? When something sounds too good to be true, it is."

"I thought you might say that. And maybe you're right. So go ahead and finish your ham. Go on and kill Milk. Rot in prison for another ten years before they shoot you up with a load of potassium chloride. Won't be my loss."

"Military death penalties are automatically appealed," Reed said. "They're appealing mine right now. The sentence could be lifted. Why would I throw that away and trust you?"

He shrugged. "You were ready to throw it away to kill an underweight pervert. But fine. If that's how you feel, appeal your sentence. Take life in prison instead. You're not yet thirty, the next fifty years should glide right by."

A knot twisted deep inside Reed's stomach, and he rubbed his thumb against the tabletop. His breath was short and shallow, like he was inhaling and exhaling through a straw. "All right, fine. Explain yourself."

"There's nothing to explain. I work for a powerful man who has the resources to restore your freedom. Somebody in this prison doesn't deserve to be alive, and that's a problem for my employer. You fix his problem, and he'll fix yours."

"So, you want me to murder somebody in cold blood?"

"No. I want you to execute justice. Just like you did in Baghdad. Just like you were about to do with Milk. I want you to be the hand of long-overdue karma."

Reed dropped the fork and wiped his mouth on a greasy section of paper towel. He folded the napkin and laid it on the table, smoothing it against the stainless steel as he noticed its flower pattern contrasting sharply with the scratches in the metal. He studied the faded blues and yellows as prisoners around the mess hall began to shuffle into line. COs barked commands. The racket felt unimportant, as though it were happening on the other side of the world.

Reed whispered between his teeth, "Who do you want me to kill?"

A smile spread across the man's thin lips. "Now that's a good question. But you need to sleep on it,

Reed. When I know you're fully committed . . . then we'll talk."

He stood and shuffled off, leaving Reed sitting alone. A CO grabbed Reed by the arm, dragging him to his feet and shoving him toward the line of men. Still, the noise was distant. Irrelevant. One thought rang through Reed's tired mind: *I can be free.*

5

Rock Hollow Penitentiary

W eeks dragged by in a muddled blur. Each day
was the same: Up before sunrise to march out
to the yard and stand in line while the COs counted
them off. If there had been any infractions from any
prisoner the day before, they would be forced to exercise. Sometimes they would be left to stand for an hour,
huddled in the cold while the COs did whatever it was
COs spent their long days doing. Then they would be
shoved into the showers.

Midday was consumed with prison housekeeping
duties, while the afternoon was contained within the
confines of the cell block, and nighttime hours were
restricted to individual cells. Usually, the guards would
let them out for an hour or so in the yard right after
lunch, but sometimes an entire day would slip by
without leaving the prison block.

The short man had vanished like a ghost. Reed

spent days searching for him amid the crowd of prisoners and uniformed guards, but he was gone as quickly and suddenly as he appeared. Stiller had never seen him before and gave Reed a twisted frown when he asked. None of the other prisoners would talk to Reed. They avoided him like the plague, knotting around Milk in the yard and giving Reed long, foreboding glares.

"They're plotting," Stiller warned. "Probably because of the shower fight. Milk was banged up pretty good. He can't lose rep over you."

The wind that howled over the high block walls brought spits of snow with it. Reed leaned against the chain-link fence and folded his arms, watching the goons across the yard. Milk sat in the midst of them, his eyes flashing death at Reed. Without a word, the pale prisoner lifted a long index finger and ran it slowly across his throat.

"Bastard," Reed whispered.

"You need allies, man," Stiller said. "The COs won't do anything until there's a fight. By then, it could be too late."

Reed stared Milk down as he adjusted his feet against the hard-packed dirt of the yard. Neither man blinked.

Stiller sighed and leaned against the fence, facing through the chain link to the next prison yard. "What's your deal, Reed? You're dark, man. Like there's a hurricane just beating you to pieces from the inside."

Reed spat into the dirt without taking his eyes off of Milk. "This is prison, Stiller. It's a pretty dark place."

"Right. But it's like . . . you're not accepting it. You're *here*, man. You're in prison. Own it. Stop making it so hard on yourself."

"I'm not staying."

Stiller shot him a sideways look. "Say what?"

Reed folded his arms. "One way or another, I'm not wasting away behind these walls."

"Dude." Stiller lifted his eyes heavenward as if he were employing supernatural assistance. "*This* is what I'm talking about. You're in denial or something. I'm not judging, but it's not real, man. This prison *is*. Do you understand me? You're in prison."

Reed watched Milk saunter across the yard, pretending to ignore the ex-Marine that was glaring daggers at him.

"Just tell me why. Explain why you're the exception."

Reed wrapped his fingers around the chain link and spoke through gritted teeth. "Because I did the right thing. The men I killed were murderers, thieves, and rapists, and that's why they died. I went to Iraq to prosecute justice, and the government didn't bat an eye at the body count until Americans started falling. And you know what? To hell with them. But I'm going to keep fighting this thing until I get out."

Stiller stared at him through tired, exhausted eyes, and shook his head. "You're not a prosecutor, Reed. Let alone a judge and jury."

"You're right. I'm not. Not like the people who put me here. I'm the kind of prosecutor nobody wants to admit that everyone needs."

Silence hung between them, their eyes still locked. With every passing moment, that silence felt heavier.

"Number 4371! Fall out!"

The voice boomed from across the yard, breaking the tension between them. Stiller shot Reed another exhausted look then shuffled off toward the fence line, leaving Reed to march across the yard toward the CO.

"Come on, con. Your attorney's here."

The CO led Reed down a hallway, through the cellblock, and into a small and windowless room on the third level. A table sat in the middle, with metal chairs on either side while a flickering yellow light buzzed from overhead, washing the room in an uneven glow.

"Sit. He'll be here shortly."

The guard snapped handcuffs around Reed's wrists, then left him alone. A chill washed through him. The bite of winter cut straight through the block walls, coating the prison in frosty discomfort. Reed could only imagine what his cell would feel like in the summer months.

The door groaned on its hinges, and a tall man in a crisp brown uniform shirt stepped in. A Marine Corps judge advocate—similar to a lawyer—here to represent Reed during the appeals process. He wore round glasses and the kind of detached, disinterested expression of a man who was already done with his day. The judge advocate set his briefcase on the table, then sat down without a word. He opened the case and shuffled through a stack of papers, spending a full five minutes scanning the file before he looked up.

My God. He hasn't even reviewed my case yet.

"You're Reed Montgomery?"

Reed nodded once, interlacing his fingers and laying his hands on the table.

The attorney returned to the papers and proceeded to read again, then folded and shoved them back into the briefcase. "I'm Lieutenant Graves, your appeals council."

"What happened to Lieutenant O'Hara?"

"She was reassigned. I'll be representing you for now."

"*For now?*"

Graves pushed the glasses up his nose. "The appeals process will be lengthy. It's possible I may be reassigned as well. Don't worry. We'll find somebody to replace me."

Reed sat back in the chair. "Okay. So what happens next?"

"Right. Well, first we'll file a motion of appeals on your sentence, then—"

"Wait. *File* a motion? You mean the motion hasn't been filed yet?"

Graves tilted his head, staring at the wall as though he'd just been asked to solve a trigonometry problem. Then he dug through the case again, shuffling through the papers. Half of them spilled onto the floor, and he didn't bother to pick them up.

"Um, no. I don't think so."

"You don't *think so?* Lieutenant, this is my life you're playing with."

The lieutenant's blue eyes flashed, blazing into a sudden glare. "You'd do well not to use that tone with me, Reed. I'm the only friend you've got. It's a lengthy process, okay? If we do well, we should have you in court within eighteen to twenty-four months, then we—"

"*Two years*? Are you kidding me?"

Once more, the perplexed frown washed over Graves's serious features. "I'm not kidding. It's not a joke."

Reed lowered his face into his hands and rubbed his thumbs into his temples. Another headache, an all-too-familiar plague, settled into the base of his skull.

"Don't worry, Reed." Graves scooped the pages off the floor and began to cram them back into the brief-case. "I'll file that appeal right away. We'll get this thing moving again. One of the Supreme Court judges is getting old. With luck, by the time we make it that far, we'll have an anti-capital punishment justice on the Court. That could be a game changer."

Reed clenched his fingers around the edge of the table. "Wait. You're already planning a Supreme Court appeal?"

Graves snapped the case shut and smiled a tight, awkward smile. "Well, Reed. The reality is the judges between here and the Supreme Court aren't very lenient. We'll do what we can, of course, but we have to be realistic. I'll see in you in a few weeks, okay?"

Graves shuffled to the door and let himself out.

Reed's heart hammered in his chest, and the room shrank around him, becoming at once stuffier than it was moments before. The flickering yellow light went out, and he laid his head on folded arms.

They've abandoned me. It's already over.

The floor felt unstable beneath his feet, as though the entire prison were swaying beneath him.

The door opened again. Reed waited for the hand of the CO to close around his shoulder, to pull him up and away from the table and back to the narrow cell he now called home. Back under the watchful eyes of Milk and his minions. At this rate, Reed would never make it to the appeals court. Milk's henchmen would mob him long before.

"Isn't he a gem?"

Reed sat up with a jolt at the familiar soft voice. The short man with nine fingers stood on the other side of the table. This time he wasn't wearing the white coveralls of a prisoner, but a brown pinstripe suit and a beige tie, complete with a pocket square poking out of the breast pocket. His close-cropped hair was gelled and combed to one side, glistening over his bright eyes.

"You!" Reed snapped. "Who the hell are you?"

The man slid into the opposite chair as Reed looked out for the guard, but the door was closed, and the room quiet.

"I'm here to discuss my proposal."

"You're not a prisoner," Reed said.

"No, I'm not. Do you want to be?"

Reed heard his own breath hissing between his lips. Each inhale tasted dry, and each exhale sour. The blood pumping through his neck surged toward his brain, clarifying the moment and driving back the confusion and questions. It didn't matter who this man was. It didn't matter what he wanted. The answer to his simple question was just as simple.

"No," Reed said. "I don't want to be a prisoner."

"What *do* you want to be, Reed?"

Reed ran his tongue over dry lips then clenched his fists. "The hand of overdue karma."

The man's smile kindled a fire of dark flames in his eyes. "Now, that's something I can help with."

6

"You have twenty-four hours. His name is Paul Choc."

From outside his cell on the second-floor landing, Reed surveyed the block. Small knots of prisoners stood scattered around the first and second floors, talking in low whispers and swapping various paraphernalia: candy, magazines, stamps.

The guards at the main entrance paced a short path back and forth in front of the door, tapping their nightsticks against their thighs while surveying the prisoners the way a man might survey week-old leftovers in the fridge. Every few minutes, one of them would yell, correcting some minor infraction. Other than the murmur of voices and occasional shouts, the block was relatively quiet—a welcome break in a busy afternoon.

Twenty-four hours. I've already blown three.

Back in his cell, Reed held his hand under the sink faucet, cupping a swallow of water in his worn palms. It tasted crisp and bitter, laden with chlorine and God knew what else.

"Stiller . . . You know a guy named Choc?"

His cellmate sat on the bunk, legs crossed under him as he flipped through an outdated magazine and shook his head without looking up.

Reed waited for a moment, then slouched against the wall, forcing himself to appear casual. "Paul Choc. I think he's housed here. Was a buddy of mine."

Stiller grunted, then flipped the magazine around. "Dude, check out the jugs on this one."

The magazine was dirty and worn with smudged fingerprints on every page.

Reed lifted an eyebrow. "Still . . . that's a cooking magazine."

Stiller laughed. "Right? Who knew cooks could be this hot."

Reed wiped his mouth with the back of his hand and cleared his throat. "So about my friend. I'd like to find him."

"I don't know a Choc. But most guys here have nicknames. What's he look like?"

I asked the same thing.

"He has a tattoo on his left forearm. An eagle with burning wings."

The magazine crackled as Stiller twisted the dry pages into a tight roll and shoved it under his shirt, scratching his back with short strokes of his muscled arms. "Blazer. I've seen him."

Reed's heart rate quickened, and he tried to remain calm, still leaning against the wall. "Where?"

Stiller cocked his head and ran his index finger

under his lip, picking at a chunk of food stuck in his back teeth. "Hmm . . . I don't know, man. It's been a while. Think maybe he got out. Or maybe they moved him to another block."

"Did he have any friends? Anyone he talked to?"

"Friends . . . hmm. I mean, I guess he hung out with the other chicos. But again, it's been a while."

"Chicos?"

"Yeah, man. The Latinos."

"Choc is Latino?"

Shit. Why did I say that?

Stiller shot him a confused frown. "I thought this guy was your friend."

Reed attempted a casual shrug. "I mean, yeah, I guess I just don't think about that kind of thing."

Stiller's frown intensified. "You good, man? This isn't about yesterday, is it? You know, I've been thinking about what you said, and—"

Reed waved his hand dismissively. "Don't worry about it, Still. I don't want to talk about it."

He stepped back out of the cell and scanned the crowd of inmates. Most were white or black. Milk and his crew slouched in one corner, talking in low voices while staring at each other through half-closed eyes—doped up on something, it seemed. Another pass of the packed cellblock, and Reed settled on the small group of prisoners sitting on the floor in one corner, playing cards with a worn-out deck. These men were slightly shorter than the rest, with olive skin and thick, dark hair.

Gotcha.

Stiller lay still on his bunk, his chest rising and falling in a smooth rhythm, and Reed slipped up beside him, running his hand along the side of the bunk and feeling between the bed frame and the mattress. Two more passes and he felt the soft edge of something that wasn't cloth or metal. Watching Stiller for any sign of a disturbance in his breathing, Reed gently lifted the mattress and pulled at the edge of the object. A moment later, he produced a small envelope from beneath the sheet, and a quick survey of its contents produced two dozen stamps, a five-dollar bill, and a couple baseball cards. Reed dumped everything into his pocket, then returned the envelope.

The Latinos looked up as Reed approached, surveying him through narrow, suspicious eyes. Trying to remain relaxed and slumping his shoulders, Reed walked slowly toward their small crowd. There were six guys, all fit and trim, with a definite aura of confidence about them. Even the smallest sat with a straight back and a bold, unwelcoming glare.

"You guys got room for one more?"

The dealer leaned against the wall, his knees propped up at chest level as he shuffled the cards. His brown fingers moved like lightning, cutting the deck twice before shuffling again. "Move along, man. We don't want nothing to do with your drama."

Pretending to be surprised, Reed frowned and looked behind him as if he were trailing some invisible baggage. He tilted his head back and nodded. "Oh, you mean that shit in the shower bay. Yeah, that wasn't my choice, man. You know how it is. . . . Gotta stick up for yourself."

"Yeah, well, stick up for yourself someplace else. Table's full."

Reed dug the stamps out of his pocket, then tapped the roll against his leg, rubbing his thumb over the glossy surface of the American flag. "You sure?"

The small crowd exchanged glances, then one of them grunted, "Let him play, Rigo."

The dealer motioned to the floor. "Ante is five flags. You won't last long."

Reed dumped five stamps onto the floor and accepted a hand of cards. They played without a sound, shuffling bets back and forth as the dealer flipped cards onto the bare floor. Reed's first hand was a bust, and he dumped more stamps onto the ground as new cards circulated the group.

"I'm Reed," he said.

Rigo snorted. "Nobody cares, man."

A round of betting passed through the circle. Two cards landed face-up. A couple players folded, and Reed dropped the five-dollar bill in the circle, resulting in raised eyebrows from the other players. The dealer flipped another two cards, and Reed dropped his to the floor. Low curses punctuated snorts of disgust as Reed shoveled the pot into his lap and sorted through the assortment of stamps, coins, and cigarettes.

"I'm looking for a friend of mine. Short dude, eagle tattoo. Goes by Blazer."

The circle fell deathly silent. Reed resisted the urge

to look up as he finished sorting the loot, then dumped five fresh stamps into the middle of the floor.

Rigo began to hand out cards, slower this time, while staring at Reed. "This ain't the lost-and-found, man. If you're looking for a friend, you can look elsewhere."

More cards hit the floor. Reed tossed fresh collateral into the pile, barely looking at his cards as he bet. The first flop passed, then the second. Once again, Reed scooped the pile into his lap. Fresh curses and glares rippled through the group, and one man tossed his cards onto the floor before shuffling off.

"I think you know him." Reed pushed a cigarette into his mouth and chewed the filter, rolling the smoke between his teeth.

"Is that right?"

"Yep. And I think you know where he is. So, what's the big secret?"

Another round of sharp, suspicious glares circulated.

The dealer shoved the cards into a tight stack and leaned forward. "Who the hell are you, man?"

Without looking up, Reed continued chewing on the smoke while sorting through his pile of winnings. "I'm just a guy who'd rather serve his time with a friend around. Don't see what the big issue is."

Rigo leaned back. "Blazer is nobody's friend. If you knew him, you know that."

Reed shrugged and checked his cards. His hand was weaker this time, which was good; a third straight win wouldn't earn him any charity from his fellow players.

"Of course not. But I still know him. He stay in this block?"

The final flop hit the floor, and the man to Reed's right scooped up the pile of winnings. A black snake tattoo rippled along his neck as he began sorting the captured loot between his knees.

"If he did, he wouldn't put up with your white ass sitting here." Snake spoke through dry lips, dropping stamps into the pot before accepting new cards from the dealer.

"So, nothing's changed?" Reed forced a laugh, trying to make it sound both strained and nervous.

I can work this angle.

Rigo tilted his head, and a slow smile spread across his tight lips. "Oh, I see. You scared, aren't you? You're making sure he's not around."

Reed shrugged. "It wouldn't break my heart if he were in another cellblock."

An alarm rang out, blasting through the block like the screech of a tornado siren. Wood clanked on metal as guards slammed their nightsticks into the bars of the lower cells.

"All right, you cons. Let's go! Back into the cells!"

Rigo scooped up the cards with a practiced flip of his fingers, shoving them back into a stack. Reed dumped his winnings into his pockets, lingering at the edge of the circle.

The playing cards clicked and hissed under Rigo's practiced fingers, and he stared across the room at the guards. "Did I see a baseball card in that pile?"

Reed flipped out the card and passed it to him. It

disappeared amid the playing cards, then into the pocket of Rigo's dirty coveralls.

"All right, man. You can sleep easy tonight. Blazer is housed in E Block. They moved him over there after a fight with some of the guys here."

Reed grunted and extended his hand. "Thanks."

Rigo glared down at the extended hand, then spat on the floor next to Reed's feet. "Get back to your cell, man. And don't come down here no more. We don't want any of your white-ass drama."

Without another word, Rigo disappeared into his cell. A hard nightstick rapped against Reed's shoulder, and one of the guards snapped from behind.

"Move it, 4371. Lights out in ten!"

Reed stomped back up the steps, casting a quick look back as he went. At the end of the cellblock, beneath the roofline high above, a narrow window provided light and a limited view of the yard outside. Just past the main rec field, a tall fence topped with razor wire separated the yard from the one next to it. Across that small field, nestled next to another fence, was an identical block building, topped with an A-frame roof. It was dark and brooding, with a short row of bold letters painted on the exterior wall: CELL-BLOCK E.

As he settled into his bed, Reed allowed himself to embrace a moment of confidence. This could be his chance—a one in a million shot at freedom. The government would give him life behind bars, at best. He remembered the short man in the pinstripe suit—his suave appearance and quiet confidence.

"*Don't question yourself, Reed. Paul Choc deserves to die. You have the opportunity to execute justice for his victims, and we have the power to reward you for it.*"

Reed closed his eyes and relaxed. He was going to do it. He was going to prosecute the man they called Blazer.

7

"You seen my stamps, man?"

Reed lay on the bottom bunk. The underside of Stiller's mattress was brown, stained, and sagged in the middle. The thin outlines of support wires that crossed on the other side of the fabric were barely strong enough to keep the abused mattress from collapsing onto the bottom bunk.

"Something dropped off your bed last night. I don't know what it was."

Stiller hopped down from his bunk and poked his head under Reed's. A moment later he reappeared with a small pile of stamps and folded bills clamped between his fingers. Reed had already removed the cigarettes but couldn't do anything about the missing cash or baseball card.

Stiller counted the collection twice, scratched behind one ear, then shrugged and replaced it beneath his pillow.

Redirecting his attention to the bottom of the

mattress, Reed studied the crisscross lines of wires. He chewed his bottom lip, twisting his fingers beneath his head.

Ten hours. I have less than ten hours.

"Hey, Still. Do the guys from E Block ever come over here?"

Stiller was busy shoving his inflated treasure back into the envelope. "I dunno, man. E Block is for the troublemakers. Surprised they haven't sent you over there."

I could stir up more trouble and make them send me over there. But I don't have time for a visit to solitary in between.

Reed pulled one of the smokes from his pocket and stuck it between his lips, biting into the paper and sucking the flavor of the nicotine out of the dry tobacco.

"Their yard is next to ours," Reed said. "Nothing but a chain-link fence separating us. You have to see them during rec sometimes."

Stiller shook his head. "I told you, man. They're troublemakers. Guards never let them out at the same time as us."

Reed suppressed a curse and closed his eyes. *There has to be a way.*

"Do they ever transfer guys over to E Block? I mean, temporarily?"

Stiller flopped back onto his bunk and unrolled the same cooking magazine, starting at page one. "Dude, I don't know. Why do you care so much about E Block? Trust me, you don't wanna be over there."

Reed sank his teeth deeper into the cigarette, cutting through the paper and exposing the tobacco. The sting of the drug seeped onto his tongue, and he imagined the vapor filling his lungs, flooding his body, and bringing welcome relief. What he wouldn't have given for a lighter. Of course, no lighters were allowed —no fire of any kind—making the cigarettes an odd and pointless commodity in the strange and volatile marketplace of prison trade.

Just a little flame. Just enough to light up an ember and generate a good cloud of smoke.

Reed's eyes snapped open. He stood up and flipped the cigarette into the toilet, then walked to the closed cell door, peering out and up toward the ceiling. He could see the air vents lined up high above, pouring warm air into the dank prison block. Far below, on the first floor, nestled in the corner next to the main gate, another grill was bolted to the blocks. But this one wasn't a vent; it was an air return where all the smelly, used air was sucked out and filtered through the climate control unit before being pumped back into each cellblock.

Reed wrapped his fingers around the bars, his eyes fixed on the air return. For the first time since being shoved off the prison bus, the tension faded from his stomach, and his muscles relaxed.

Perfect.

Darkness descended over the prison, broken only by the systematic rhythm of boots as the guards conducted their circuits. Reed lay awake on the bottom bunk, listening to Stiller snore. As the minutes drained into hours, the snores became deeper and more relaxed, blending with the creak of the wind against the metal roof far above.

Every twenty minutes, a CO passed the entrance to their cell, casting a lazy glance over the occupants before moving on. Reed lay perfectly still, counting each second in his mind and matching the beat of the boots with the tick of a nonexistent clock. The method wasn't perfect, and neither were the circuits. Sometimes the CO would pass five minutes early, and sometimes ten minutes late. Sometimes his boots rang sharp and clear against the floor, and sometimes he slipped up in front of the cell with a lazy creep that was all but silent.

Reed didn't think the tactical advantages of this irregular method were intentional. More than likely, the CO was simply tired and bored and conducting his job at random to keep himself awake. Either way, it made Reed's task that much harder.

Slipping his fingers under the thin sheets, Reed felt along the edge of his cheap commercial mattress. It was made entirely of foam, but not the fancy kind. More like the kind you find in the seat of a tractor: thick, yellow, and spongy, encased in a thick waterproof sleeve that looked like the tarpaulins FEMA spreads over busted roofs after a hurricane. Along the bottom edge of the mattress, a seam ran in the tarp, manufactured of rough stitches and plastic rolled on top of itself in a thick strip. As Reed ran his hand along the seam, he twisted the plastic beneath his fingers, gratified to find it stiff and inflexible—a little too inflexible for plastic alone.

The swish of pant legs echoed down the balcony. Reed froze and closed his eyes, waiting for the guard to pass. He counted to a hundred just to be certain, then rolled sideways and leaned over the side of the bed. The plastic tasted like sweat, grime, and pure body odor between his teeth. He bit down on the seam, grinding it in his mouth with increasing pressure and pulling on the plastic with both hands. His stomach convulsed, and he wanted to vomit, but he kept chewing—another bite, and then a twist. The plastic tore and slid back, exposing a thin wire core as thick as a coat hanger, but more flexible.

Reed spat plastic and saliva and twisted his fingers around the wire. It was perfect—malleable but strong —and made out of cheap steel. He slipped his fingers into the hole of the plastic and tore it back, exposing a wide section of dirty yellow foam and several inches of the wire. Careful pressure with his fingers caused the wire to bend around the bed frame. Reed rolled the wire and bent it in the opposite direction, back and forth, until it finally snapped under the heat and friction. He tore the seam another few feet down the length of the mattress, masking the ripping of the plastic with Stiller's violent snores, then repeated the process of bending the wire until he broke off a three-foot section. It was flimsy in his hands, but the weight and strength were sufficient. He coiled the wire around his fingers, being careful not to bend it too harshly, then slipped it into his pocket.

The foam felt as dirty as it looked, sticking to his fingers as he pulled it apart. Little chunks broke free of the mattress and filled his hands, leaving smudges of grease and grime on his palms. Reed pressed handfuls of the petroleum product into his jumpsuit, packing it in around his waist. It was hot and sticky next to his body and filled his nostrils with the stench of more body odor. He wrinkled his nose and zipped the coveralls shut, then rested his head against the pillow.

A full six hours remained between him and the morning wakeup call, and eight hours left until the deadline.

It has to be enough.

The cell door shrieked back on its hinges, grinding under the whine of the electric motor. Reed's eyes snapped open, and he propped himself up on his elbows. The lights that snapped on blazed without the familiar scream of COs shouting, *"Lights! Lights!"*

Something was wrong.

The footsteps that filled the air like the rumble of a freight train were much louder than usual. Dozens of metallic shrieks ripped through the silence as more cell doors were electrically opened, followed by the squeal of the intercom from the ceiling high above.

"All prisoners, fall out! Assemble on ground level! Fall out!"

Reed peered out over the railing to the lower level, where no less than forty COs gathered around the bottom units and shoved prisoners out of their beds and onto the floor. Another twenty guards were pounding their way directly toward him.

"What's this?" Reed shouted.

Stiller stumbled out of bed, yawning. "Shakedown, dude. They do it once or twice a month. Checking for contraband."

Shakedown. Shit.

"All prisoners! *Fall out!*"

Stiller hit the floor. "Let's go, man. Get to the ground floor."

The mattress was barely covered by the blanket, leaving the hole where Reed had dug the foam and wire out partially exposed and easy to find.

"Dude, let's go! You don't want to be here when they are."

Reed stumbled out onto the balcony, his legs feeling suddenly wobbly. He joined the long line of sleepy prisoners, listening to the guards shouting and turning the cells upside down. As he stepped off the stairs and onto the main floor, Milk caught him by the arm. "I'm coming for you, bitch."

Reed jerked away and pressed into the crowd of prisoners gathering around the far end of the cellblock. Most looked half-awake, only half wore shoes, and the fat ones had their coveralls tied around their waists, exposing broad and sweaty chests.

"Let's go, cons! Against the wall!"

Reed forced his way to the back of the crowd, feeling his shoulders rammed against the blocks as the entire population of the cellblock pushed him backward. He inched his way sideways along the wall, feeling with his right hand until his fingers closed around a hard metal edge—the frame of the air return.

The leg of his coveralls clung to the surface of the vent as the heating unit sucked sordid air back into the conduits. Like the rest of the prison, the surface of the grate was grimy to the touch, but there was a full one-inch gap between the slats. Reed pushed himself downward, kneeling against the wall before he dug inside his coveralls. The noise inside the cellblock became deafening—a combination of shouting guards and grumbling prisoners. The suffocating smell of body odor was overwhelming at this height, but nobody noticed him. Nobody looked down as Reed shoved wads of mattress foam between the slats and into the mouth of the air return.

Where are the Latinos? I need the Latinos.

He pressed the last wad of foam through the grill and stood up again. Nobody had noticed, but when he looked down at the grill, the pile of foam was clearly visible. Smaller chunks of the mattress had already disappeared inside the conduit, sucked away by the pressure of the returning air, but a sizable mound remained behind, lying just on the other side of the slats.

Reed grabbed the nearest prisoner by the sleeve and gave it a soft jerk. "Hey, where are the Latinos?"

The big man glared at him, then jerked the sleeve free and stumbled off. Fighting his way through the packed crowd, Reed shoved elbows and thick arms aside as he searched for the shorter crowd of men from the day before. The shout of guards and grumble of the prisoners grew louder in his ears, pounding in a constant chorus. Each breath of the filthy prison clogged his lungs.

Reed saw the ringleader first: short with curly black hair and wiry brown arms—the stuff of south LA— every bit the hardened gangster. He pushed through two more half-naked convicts and tugged on Rigo's sleeve. "Amigo."

The short man spun on him. "Who you calling *amigo*, gringo?"

Reed brushed the bluster aside and leaned down to make himself heard over the ruckus. "I need your lighter. You can have everything from yesterday. Everything I won."

Rigo wrapped his fingers into fists and took a step back. "I don't know what you're talking about, white boy, but you better clear out of here before I put a hurt on your ass."

Reed gritted his teeth. "Look, *dude*. Nobody carries that many smokes without a flame. I know you've got one, and I know you've got it on you. You wouldn't leave it in your cell during a shakedown."

Rigo shook his head. "Move along, man. If you know what's good for you—"

"*Number 4371!*" The voice boomed out from the second floor, cascading over the crowd with all the terror of a direct thunderclap. Reed's mouth went dry. A guard stood outside his cell, bellowing into a bullhorn. The man's face blazed red, and he searched the crowd below him.

"Number 4371! *Fall out!*"

"Oh no, white boy." Rigo's lips twisted into a smirk. "Looks like you got busted."

Panicked adrenaline surged through Reed's body. He whirled back around and grabbed Rigo by the neck, pulling him in close before driving his fist full force into the Latino's jaw. Bone met bone with a sharp crack, and blood sprayed across Reed's white jumpsuit. Somebody shouted, and chaos erupted.

Reed grabbed the collar of Rigo's jumpsuit and ripped it open, pulling it down over his shoulder before running his hand down Rigo's back and feeling between his butt cheeks. His fingers closed around the hard edge of the lighter. Though barely conscious, Rigo spluttered and tried to fight. Reed swept his feet out from under him, then turned and launched himself back into the crowd. The COs shouted. The bullhorn blared. Every noise bounced and echoed off the bare walls as though the entire prison were caught in a giant blender, and Reed was slipping toward the blades.

He slid to his knees at the grate, ground his finger against the wheel of the Zippo lighter, and waited for the flame to dance. The metal fins of the air grate sliced into his skin, drawing blood as he pressed the lighter through the vent and onto the pile of greasy petroleum foam.

Bright light and heat washed over Reed's face,

singeing his eyebrows and sending him stumbling backward. He fought to regain his balance, but his right foot slipped, and he crashed onto his tailbone as fresh clouds of smoke billowed into the air return.

"Number 4371! Show us your hands!"

8

The snarling, acne-covered guard closed his hand around Reed's arm, but Reed pulled himself free, launching himself back into the crowd and hiding amid the packed prisoners as the COs closed in on all sides. The bullhorn barked, and fresh guards burst into the cellblock. Reed ducked and tried to push himself farther into the crowd, but the attempt was futile; there was no more room to move.

Reed tipped his head back, gazing at the ceiling where rows of AC vents lined the exposed ductwork. A trace of smoke escaped the suck of the air return, wafting toward the ceiling. A moment later, the shrieking ring of the fire alarm overtook the blare of the bullhorn. Red lights flashed from the ceiling, and panic overwhelmed the entire prison.

"Fall into line. *Fall in, convicts!*"

Reed pressed himself behind a short man with one ear, ducking low to avoid detection. The COs crowded around the prisoners, shoving them toward the hallway that led into the yard and pushing them along with snapping shouts and the crack of nightsticks against concrete.

"Evacuate Block D! All convicts, move into the yard!"

The commands were barely audible over the scream of the alarm. Ducking and stumbling through the door and into the yard, Reed shielded himself against the mass of swinging body parts around him. The yard was still clothed in the inky black of the early morning hours. Even the spotlights of the towers were directed elsewhere, back onto the roof of Block D as the guards searched for the source of the smoke.

Reed turned away from the crowd and walked toward the fence near E Block's yard. He waited, drumming his knuckles against his thigh as he stared at the sister block standing tall and dark under the black sky. The moments that ticked by felt like hours. He placed his hand against the chain-link and dug his toes into the mud. The air smelled crisp and clean, but there was still the undertone of dirty bodies from the cage designed to house them all until the end of time.

Red lights flashed from the upper windows of the cellblock, and another fire alarm shrieked, this one ringing from inside E Block's walls. An unknown thrill, a rush he had never felt before, washed through his veins. It wasn't excitement or even nervousness; it was vindication—the sort of self-justice you feel when against all odds, you got something right.

Prisoners poured out of E Block. They stumbled into one another, groggy and confused, leaning forward and rubbing their eyes as a smaller group of COs evacuated them. They dispersed into the yard, looking for places to sit while they awaited their return to bed. Reed scanned each face in the crowd, searching for any sign of a Latino, checking every arm for the eagle tattoo. Because of the white jumpsuits, most arms were obscured from view, and those that were exposed were too wreathed in shadow to be discernible.

Then he saw him: short with bulging muscles and a bald head, his sleeves torn off, revealing thick arms covered in tattoos. On the left one, just beneath his elbow, was the feathery face of a screaming bald eagle wreathed in fire.

Reed reached into his pocket and closed his fingers around the wire, lifting it out and unwinding it, leaving the strand hanging at his left side in a gently curved strip. "Blazer!"

The muscular Latino looked up immediately, squinting through the yard lights, and took a half step forward.

Reed called again. "Blazer, don't you remember me?"

Another few yards closed. His face was scarred, betraying the hardened features of a longtime resident of the prison. He stopped five feet from the fence and glowered at Reed. "Who the hell are you, man?"

Reed forced a laugh. "Dude, it's me. Travis. From back home?"

Blazer took another step toward the fence.

The gaps in the chain-link were just large enough for Reed to slip his wrist through, and he held out his hand, fingers open, waiting to shake. "Blazer. . . . Don't break my heart, man. I don't have friends around here."

The Latino squinted and leaned forward another two inches. It was two inches close enough.

Reed shot his arm through the barrier and dug his fingers into the collar of Blazer's jumpsuit, then pulled him in until his head crashed against the chain-link fence. With a flip of his left wrist, Reed ran the wire through the fence and around Blazer's neck, catching the tail end with his right hand and pulling it back through the chain-link. Blazer twisted and shouted as he tried to break free. He twisted on his feet, turning until he faced away from Reed.

It was a fatal mistake.

With the wire closed around his throat, Reed pulled back and jerked right in one powerful motion. The wire sliced right through the skin and cut through Blazer's windpipe, sending a spray of blood over the loose gravel as Reed finished the stroke and released the wire. Blazer collapsed to the ground, and Reed stumbled backward. His hands were sticky, now coated with a thin layer of blood. Blazer choked and thrashed, his hands flying to his throat as his panicked eyes stared at the sky. Several of the other E Block inmates shouted and rushed toward him, but the damage was already done.

Blazer choked out in just over a minute, his dead eyes still staring heavenward.

What the hell have I done?

For the first time, Reed thought of cameras. Guards posted on surveillance. Other prisoners. Who might have seen him? He fell to his knees and began to grind dirt against his palms, rubbing away the gunky crimson of death. He was only vaguely aware of other prisoners shouting and running away from the prison block. Every noise and sensation was dampened, muted by the reality sinking into his bones.

I just killed a man.

"Well, what do we have here? A little bitch, all by himself."

Reed scrambled to his feet and whirled around. Two big men stood behind Milk, only ten yards away. Rigo appeared out of the crowd to join them, his lips lifted into a deadly snarl.

Mud crumbled beneath his bare feet as Reed stumbled back, kicking out and swinging with his left hand. He missed, and Rigo darted in, sending a swift kick to his stomach. The world spun, and Reed lashed out, connecting with somebody's face before a sharp object sliced into his arm, followed by another blow to his wounded stomach. The leering sneer of the cross-eyed Hulk appeared in the corner of his eye just before a massive, meaty fist came crashing down, straight into the base of Reed's skull.

The greasy smell of the room reminded Reed of hydraulic fluid or engine oil. It was distinct. Heavy. It didn't smell like the prison. His arms, neck, and most of all, his skull hurt as he fought for consciousness. Agony washed over him, the claws of a dragon digging into his flesh and ripping the muscles straight off the bone.

"Give him another."

Like the bite of an insect, something stung his arm and burrowed into his skin. Warmth flooded his blood, and his mind began to clear. He could see a dim light in the otherwise dark room with metal walls and that thick, greasy smell. He sat in a chair, unrestrained at a metal table. Two men bustled around behind him, and two more sat on the far side of the table. He recognized the man on the left immediately. It was the short, stocky man from the prison. The one who vanished then reappeared in the brown pinstripe suit. He didn't know the second man, tall and lean, with a carefully trimmed beard and not a hair on his scalp. His green eyes flashed, and the stub of a cigar glowed between his fingers.

I didn't smell the cigar.

It was such an odd thought, such a pointless thing to notice, especially since he smelled it now—thick and sweet.

"Welcome to the land of the living, Number 4371."

Sarcasm tainted the familiar voice of the man on the left. Out of his pinstripe suit, he now wore a tight black T-shirt and silver chain necklace with a dangling golden crucifix.

Reed raised his fingers to his face, rubbing his tired eyes. "Where am I?"

"Right where I promised you'd be. You're on the outside, Reed. You're free."

The fight outside the prison. The staged fire. The

feeling of the wire slicing through skin as it tore into Blazer's throat. A sick feeling settled into his stomach as every detailed memory flooded back into the forefront of his mind.

"You're wondering how you did it."

For the first time, the man on the right spoke. His English had just a hint of refined London drawl. He looked to be in his late fifties, Reed thought, with a mostly white beard and some wrinkles, but his eyes were still strong. Still potent.

"That's always the question," the man continued. "*How did I do it? How did I kill a man in cold blood?*"

Everything felt as though it were happening in slow motion, just quick enough for Reed to make sense of one action as it related to another.

"I'll tell you how you did it, Reed. You did it because it's who you are. You're a born killer. A natural wielder of justice. That's how you killed those contractors in Iraq, isn't it? Because they deserved to die. And that's how you'll kill your next dozen targets, too."

The words rang clearer now, and the mental fog began to fade. "Who the hell are you?"

"My name is Oliver Enfield. I operate an independent contracting agency. We supply professional killers for hire."

The words were so frank, so direct that Reed knew he should've felt surprised, but he didn't. The only thing he felt was confusion. "You got me out of prison?"

"I did."

"That's not possible."

"It is, and it happened. It's all a matter of influence. Something you'll come to find I have a great deal of."

"They're coming for me. Whoever you are, they're coming for you, too."

Oliver laughed. It was a deep, confident sound. Not at all uncomfortable, either. It was more like the warm chuckle your grandfather makes when you tell a cheesy joke.

"Reed, when I say it's all a matter of influence, what I mean is, *everything* is a matter of influence. Nobody is coming for you. In fact, as of this moment, nobody knows you exist. Your record is gone. The court-martial files. The prison manifest. Even your fingerprints. Like I said, I am a man of tremendous influence."

The words made sense, but they didn't quite compute. The claims were either too radical or too absurd to feel true.

"What do you want?" It was the only question Reed could think of.

Oliver took a puff on the cigar, then faced Reed dead in the eye. In an instant, all the warmth and gentleness faded from his features, replaced by cold calculation.

"I want you to do what you do best. I want you to kill. And you're going to do it for me."

The room was suddenly quiet. The man in the black T-shirt interlaced his fingers and leaned forward, staring at Reed without blinking. The goons in the background stood out of sight, also silent.

"I already did that," Reed said. "Choc is dead. I cut his throat."

"Yes. A very inventive method, I will say. We'll have to work on your subtlety—because you don't have any. But in the meantime, suffice it to say that I'm impressed."

"Okay. Good. So you let me go now like you promised. He's dead. You got me out of prison. We're done."

Oliver puffed on the cigar again. "No, Reed. We're not done. One life gets you out of prison. Thirty more *keep* you out of prison. I'm not looking for a one-time hit inside a pen full of the world's most violent killers. I could have done that myself for free. I'm looking for a lethal weapon to join my growing enterprise. Somebody ruthless. Somebody like you."

Reed clenched his hands over the table. "I'm not killing thirty people for you. He said I kill and I walk. *That was the deal!*"

Oliver exchanged glances with his companion, then ground the cigar against the tabletop. "If that's how you feel, I can have you back in prison before nightfall. They'll put you straight into solitary while they prepare a trial for the murder of Paul Choc. They don't know you did it, but I'll make sure they learn. Or maybe I won't. Maybe you won't have to worry about death row. I own half that prison. By the end of the week, you could be in a white body bag lying in the morgue."

There was no deceit in Oliver's stone-cold eyes. No bluster. This man was absolutely serious. He would kill Reed in a heartbeat, and without a second thought.

Oliver tapped his finger on the table and narrowed his eyes at Reed. "They tell me you have a word for what you did in Iraq. They say you called yourself a *prosecutor*."

Reed didn't answer. He returned the stare with as much confidence and bluster as he could muster.

"I like that word," Oliver said. "I like the spirit behind it. The idea that you can pursue justice independently of a corrupt judicial system. That's pretty much what my company does all year long." He leaned forward. "Come with me, Reed. I'll make you the scourge of a world that is long overdue the sword of justice. I'll make you rich. I'll make you terrible. I'll make you more deadly than the strongest spec ops soldier on the planet. I'll give you a home and a purpose and something to call your own. I'll make you more than free. I'll make you God. I'll make you the Prosecutor."

Reed sucked in a long breath through his nose, and the muscles in his back began to loosen. A calm swallowed his soul like the eye of a hurricane passing over a storm-battered city. It wasn't peace. It didn't feel like security. It just felt like a momentary reprieve from the blast of the storm—an opportunity to find shelter.

"Thirty kills?" he asked.

Oliver's mouth twisted into a glistening smile. "Thirty kills."

9

Three years later
43 Miles Northeast of Atlanta

Orange flames licked up the side of the cabin, racing along the darkened stains of gasoline that saturated the timbers. Sparks and pine splinters fell from the walls, raining down on the wet earth beneath. The rain that fell through the trees in a gentle shower wouldn't stop the blaze, but there was no danger of the fire being blown into the surrounding trees. Within minutes, the roof began to creak, then it collapsed into the living room amid a rush of sparks.

Baxter whimpered. His bottom teeth jutted out, and his head tilted to one side as he watched the flames. Reed patted him behind his ears, feeling the greasy hair matted between the rolls of fat that hung to the bulldog's neck.

"I know, boy," Reed whispered. "We knew it could end this way."

The dog snorted and pawed the ground, then stood up. Without a backward glance, he walked down the hill toward the pickup truck parked at the end of the driveway. Staring into the flames a moment longer, Reed watched his longtime home disintegrate. Not for the first time, his aching mind wandered back to Banks —the stunning blonde he met at a nightclub only hours before all hell broke loose and his world feel apart. He saw her eyes, her smile, the way her whole body glowed when she sang. He imagined her lips on his and remembered the way they tasted. How she felt. The way she made him feel.

He closed his eyes. Ignored the cold wind on his back conflicting with the warmth of the fire on his face. It took every ounce of willpower and determination to walk away from Banks. To leave her out of this hellish war he had fallen into. He opened his eyes and clenched his jaw. The aching in his heart to find her again, to be with her, couldn't wash away the burning reality of who he was and what he had to do. No matter how desperately he longed to hold her again, just for a moment, there was a deeper, more burning desire in his soul—a desire for vengeance.

Without another glance, Reed shouldered the backpack and started after the dog. Each step brought new resolve to his mind. New anger. For three years, he believed a lie. Believed that after thirty brutal kills, he would be a free man with nothing but a wide-open road in front of him. That was the snake oil that Oliver Enfield sold him when he shook Reed's hand and designated him *Codename Prosecutor*. Reed wanted to believe it was for real—a genuine opportunity for belonging, for something bigger than himself. But at the end of the day, that too had faded into a lie as quickly as the cabin turned to ash behind him.

Three weeks had passed since the train wreck in east Atlanta when Reed first learned that his mentor and employer had sold him out to an unknown enemy. Reed spent those weeks bouncing from one grimy hotel to another, laying low and giving his injuries as much time as possible to heal. Then he returned to his cabin to scrub the place, removing anything and everything that could be traced back to him. He packed the bulk of his gear into the trunk of the Camaro, then stashed the car in a storage shed. He paid in cash and gave the clerk a fake name and South Carolina driver's license. Nothing could be traced back to him. The FBI would search for the black Camaro last seen at the site of the Peachtree Tower. Of course, Reed removed the license plate before that operation, but the car was still too conspicuous for him to risk. The black pickup truck from the rental car company would be easier to hide in and easier to ditch if things went sideways.

And things were almost certainly about to go sideways.

He opened the door of the pickup and Baxter jumped in, landing in the passenger seat and settling down for the ride. Reed tossed the backpack in the rear seat on top of the rifle case. The pack contained his standard rush kit, loaded with everything he needed to vanish. Fake IDs, straps of cash in three different currencies, survival gear, spare burner cell phones, and enough ammunition to lay down a battalion of Marines. Or maybe a kingpin killer and his army of goons.

Gravel crunched under the tires of the truck as it bounced down the unpaved road back toward town. It took almost twenty minutes to reach the blacktop again, and Reed turned southwest toward Canton. The sun crested through the treetops, blazing through the thinning clouds and into the pickup, covering his bruised skin with welcome warmth. As the mile markers ticked by, more cars joined him on the ever-widening highway. The daily grind of metropolitan Atlanta was underway, bringing fresh bustle and noise to drown out the chaos of days before.

Baxter rested his head on his paws and stared into space. A trail of drool drained from his bottom lip and onto the seat, but he didn't snore like he usually did while relaxing. His whole body was still and quiet.

Large brick houses lined the streets of a neighborhood, complete with postage-stamp lawns, brown privacy fences, and identical Bradford pear trees. All the driveways were pressure-washed white, and the few cars that sat outside the garages were all new and clean, white and black, mostly SUVs and sport sedans with the occasional Japanese minivan mixed in. It was a quiet Caucasian neighborhood, still asleep prior to the impending rush of weekday life.

The truck squeaked to a stop in front of a home at the end of a cul-de-sac. The flowerbeds in front of the brick were packed with bright fall colors, and the lawn was clean and raked. A black sedan sat in the driveway with a blue bumper sticker plastered just beneath the left taillight: My Cat Should Be President.

Reed switched the truck off and admired the car and the house and the perfectly clean yard. It looked peaceful. Maybe not happy. Definitely not exciting. But certainly peaceful. The kind of peace that a quiet, simple, boring life promises.

He checked the gun under his unzipped jacket, then walked across the lawn and up the spotless side-walk to the front door. The neighborhood was quiet and calm, making his knuckles sound like gunshots as they collided with the door. He shoved his hands into his pockets and waited, drawing a deep breath of the fall that was much colder than a typical November morning in North Georgia.

Moments ticked by until he heard the soft patter of footsteps and then the thump of a forehead resting against the door. The peephole darkened. The chain rattled in its slot, then the bolt snapped back. The door glided open on silent, greased hinges.

Kelly wore hospital scrubs and tennis shoes, both a minty green, and her thin brown hair was swept back behind her ears. She stared into Reed's eyes with silent, reserved calmness, then sighed and stepped back. "Come in."

A tasteful assortment of accents and framed pictures hung on the walls of the home. Dim light shone from the living room, glinting off the dark-brown tile. He didn't see a cat, but a bowl labeled "kitty dinner" sat on the floor next to a water dish. Coming from someplace upstairs, Reed heard the sound of

water splashing in a shower and the muted tone of a
man singing. He pulled the coat a little tighter over the
gun and followed Kelly down the hall and into the
kitchen. With each step, uncertainty overwhelmed his
confidence. He'd never been there before, and he
hadn't seen Kelly since she patched him up after the
train wreck. Before that, it had been almost twelve
months. But the way she walked—the look in those
dark eyes—it still made his head go light. He remembered when that feeling was the only thing that got him
out of bed in the morning, but now it ignited only guilt.

Kelly led him into the kitchen, and without a word,
she filled a coffee cup from the pot and passed it to
him. Reed sipped it in silence while she propped her
elbows on the counter and calmly watched him.

"Seems like you're back on your feet, in spite of my
directions."

Reed shrugged. The hot coffee warmed his chilled
fingers.

"Leg healing up okay?"

"Yep." Through the back window, he saw a
flowerbed and a swing set, new and still glistening with
bright paint that the first summer would burn into
dullness. One child's swing with tiny straps hung from
the bar. It was yellow.

Reed turned back to Kelly and raised both
eyebrows. She nodded once but didn't say anything.

"Congratulations. I'm happy for you." He wasn't
sure if he meant those words or not. They were just
what he needed to say. The best way to stay numb was
to suppress his feelings.

"I asked you not to come around anymore, Reed. I was very clear about that." An edge crept into Kelly's tone.

"I know. It's not about the medical. I—"

A skinny man with blonde hair stepped off the staircase and into the hallway. Water dripped from his hair, and there was a towel wrapped around his waist. Steam still rose from his flushed skin, and a big smile hung on his lips. "Kelly, I was thinking—" His smile faded when he saw Reed, but there was no defensiveness in his posture—just surprise.

"John, this is Reed." Kelly poured another cup of coffee, and John stepped forward and took the coffee before extending his hand toward Reed. The grip was firm and confident, but not all that strong.

Reed shook once, then released.

"Reed is my realtor. He sold me the house." Kelly stared into her cup.

"Oh, cool." The smile returned, and John took a deep sip of the coffee. "Sorry to come down dressed like this, man. Didn't know we had company."

Reed forced a tight smile. "It's early. My intrusion."

John shifted on his feet, then flashed another nervous smile. "Well, I better get dressed. Good meeting you, Reed." He disappeared back up the steps, coffee in hand.

Reed turned back to Kelly and raised one eyebrow. She flicked her hand at him and turned away, wiping down the counter with a dry cloth.

"He seems nice," Reed said. He hoped the insincerity in his voice wasn't as obvious as John's awkwardness.

"He is."

"Is he . . . umm . . . ?"

Kelly rolled her eyes. "A Christian?"

"Well, yeah. I guess."

"Yes. I met him at church."

"I'm happy for you."

Kelly flung the cloth into the sink and shot him a glare. "You don't have to lie, Reed. I know what you think. He's not like you. He's not big and blunt and brutal. Not everyone has to be."

The room fell silent with that awkward, tense mood like an invisible fog.

Kelly leaned against the counter and wiped hair from her face. "I'm sorry."

Reed rubbed his finger over the mosaic pattern of the mug, tracing each spiral and shard of colored glass. "I never hated you for what you believe. I just don't feel the same."

"I know." She stared at the floor, and once again, the silence felt thick.

Reed imagined he could feel each second slipping by, punctuated by a heart rate that shouldn't be so pronounced. He looked into the backyard again and studied the swing. Bright yellow. Gender-neutral. The kind of thing only an overzealous future parent would buy before they even knew the sex of their child. That was Kelly, always jumping ahead.

"Why are you here, Reed?"

The sudden question jarred Reed out of his muse.

He dumped the coffee into the sink and leaned on the counter. "I need you to keep Baxter for a couple days. He's in the truck." He shoved his hands back into his pockets and rested against the kitchen island.

"I told you I was done. I'm not getting mixed up in your chaos anymore. I'm an honest woman now."

"You were always an honest woman, Kelly. That's what made you such a shitty thief."

She rolled her eyes. "I wasn't half bad in my better days."

"Does John know about your better days?"

She looked away. "What do you think?"

"I doubt he'll ever ask. Doesn't impress me as an inquisitive person."

"What about when I tell him my realtor's dog is staying the week?"

Reed grinned. "Hey, you set yourself up for that one."

Kelly's dark eyes were rimmed with red.

Reed stepped across the room and placed one hand on her arm, squeezing softly. "This is the last time. I swear to you. There's something I have to clean up, but when I'm finished, I'll come back for Baxter and then I'll be gone. You'll never see or hear from me again."

A single tear spilled out of her eye. She looked away, glaring at the back patio through the sliding glass door. "You think that's what I want?"

"I think it's what you need."

Reed brushed the fallen bangs out of her eyes, then leaned down and kissed the top of her head. He gave her arm another squeeze and then walked toward the door. "Three days, Kel. Maybe four."

"I charge for pet sitting!"

Reed paused and shot her a wink and a grin. "Maybe I'll pay off the house."

As the door closed behind him, Reed faced north toward the mountains. The breeze that stung his cheeks unleashed fresh resolve in his veins. He pushed back the thoughts of Kelly and her quiet life, and he remembered Atlanta—the wrecked train, the bloody bodies, and the ultimate backstabbing. He was only one kill away from a quiet life like this—one of retirement and solitude—or at least he thought he was. But that had all been a farce. Oliver's promise of thirty kills in exchange for his freedom was a lie from the start, and it was a lie Reed would never swallow. He worked as a professional killer under the condition that he killed people who deserved to be killed. It was a cheap, clichéd excuse for his bloody profession, but it was how he justified the relentless slaughter.

Oliver made a terrible miscalculation when he turned on Reed, failing to realize that a man they called *Prosecutor*—a man who made his living gunning down injustice—should be the last man he tried to backstab.

I'm coming for you, Oliver.

10

Western North Carolina

" . . . It's twenty-eight degrees here in beautiful Cherokee County and not showing any signs of warming up. This is truly radical weather for late November. We've got a cold front sweeping down from the Midwest, with temperatures expected to fall into the single digits overnight. You're gonna want to get home early tonight and make sure you bundle up. It's gonna be a cold one. From channel—"

Reed cut the radio off and settled back into the cloth seat of the pickup. The heater hummed on low, pumping hot air over the windshield to keep it from fogging. Even though the cab of the truck was warm, Reed could feel the chill from the other side of the glass. It hung in the trees as a semi-frozen mist, frosting over the tips of the limbs and collecting on the grass. Chunks of ice cascaded down the gurgling brooks that crisscrossed beneath the county road, and what leaves remained in the trees were stiff with the sub-freezing temperatures. The brunt of impending winter was hitting North Carolina early, and even the animals had taken shelter. The mountains felt still and silent, almost as though a brooding force lay in the shadows between the trees, waiting and watching, haunting every passerby who defied the claws of the cold.

The two-lane mountain road wound back on itself, weaving its way farther into the mountains. Every ten or fifteen minutes, another vehicle passed him, slipping by on the narrow space between the yellow lines and a hundred-yard cliff, dropping down into the depths of an empty ravine.

Reed left the town of Murphy over an hour before, skirting Hiwassee Lake before working his way through the back roads and into the wilderness. Oliver's cabin headquarters lay deep in the heart of the North Carolina Appalachians, far off the beaten path, where no hunter or hiker would ever stumble across it. Reed discovered the location by accident while reviewing kill contracts almost two years before. It was a secret, and at the time, he didn't mention it to Oliver to avoid his employer's possible wrath. Now the secret carried an entirely new value. With any luck, Oliver would be holed up in his safe house, half-drunk and sitting by the fire when Reed closed in. It was equally possible that Oliver was on the other side of the world, negotiating contracts with Indonesian warlords, but Reed was willing to take the chance that his former employer wouldn't leave the States until the Prosecutor had been put to bed. They had to know he was coming.

Reed turned off the blacktop and onto a back road. Using the GPS, he rechecked his position relative to the cabin: six miles out, separated by two ravines and one river. The river would be the greatest challenge. There was a bridge, sure, but it was an obvious point of weakness for Oliver's defenses. At two miles from the cabin, it was almost certain that the old killer had some surveillance at the bridge.

Reed would have to figure something else out when the time came. He would leave the pickup in the woods, three miles out, wait for the cover of darkness, then approach the cabin from the west. Oliver might not be alone and could have dogs or tripwires criss-crossing between the trees around the cabin. It would be a painfully slow process to make his approach, and Reed was ready to take his time.

The digital thermometer on the dash read twenty-two degrees when Reed cut off the truck fifty yards from the road, buried in the trees. He settled into the seat and waited while the heat slowly vacated the cabin, replaced by an icy temperature that seeped straight through his thick black jacket and into his bones. He rested his head back against the headrest, crossing his arms, and embraced the discomfort. It burned, then it ached. Soon his mind would numb it out, just like it had a thousand times before, and then he'd be ready to conquer the wilderness and beat it into submission.

"You are God. Everything is subject to your will. The day you stop believing that is the day you die."

Oliver's admonition rang in Reed's mind—a distant echo of three years before during his intense training. Fresh out of prison, with nothing to lose and everything to win, Reed followed Oliver into these very mountains. It was winter, snow lay on the ground, and for a Marine fresh out of Iraq, this new ice demon was an unprecedented threat. Here in these mountains, miles away from civilization, Oliver and his goons took Reed to the edge of death, forcing him through a four-month pressure-cooker course designed to remove the humanity from his soul and make him the ultimate killer.

"I'm going to destroy you. And if by some miracle you prove to be indestructible, I'm going to hire you."

Reed guessed that the challenge was meant to be horrific, but it wasn't. He'd already been on death row, so the thought of losing his life here in this frozen wilderness was less than terrifying. It was more annoying than anything because when he accepted Oliver's thirty-kill deal, he was under the impression that he *was* hired. The sudden change of events in North Carolina felt like backtracking, but these mountains hadn't killed him then, and they wouldn't kill him now.

The sun slowly faded over the western horizon, vanishing amid the trees and leaving the forest in a ghostly glow of moonlight and shadow. Reed would have preferred perfect darkness, pierced by the illumination of his night vision goggles, but there was no time to waste defying the clear sky and full moon. He would have to make do with the shadows.

Reed's wristwatch read nine thirty before he slipped out of the truck, shutting the door softly behind him. The ground was frozen, and brittle mud crunched with each footfall. Thin fog drifted down from the tree limbs, further distorting the darkness and making every shadow morph under the shine of the moon. In the distance, an owl hooted. Amid the leaves to the north, a chipmunk scampered through the forest. Or maybe it was a squirrel. The cold that cut through his jacket no longer bothered him; it felt natural to feel this numb, even with the added discomfort of a glacial breeze drifting out of the west.

I dominate this. This cold is mine.

Reed opened the back door of the truck and dug through the bags. His handgun was already strapped beneath the jacket, accompanied by two spare magazines and a Ka-Bar knife. He withdrew his custom-built AR-10 sniper rifle, chambered in .308. It was the same weapon he had wielded from the top of the Equitable Building in Atlanta a few days before. He slipped a twenty-round magazine into the receiver, then dumped two more magazines into the oversized pockets of his jacket. Last, he pulled an oversized backpack on a metal frame from the back seat and secured it to his shoulders. A black baseball cap pulled low over his ears completed his ensemble. There was too much moonlight for his nightvision goggles to be truly effective, and they would respond poorly to muzzle flash.

He'd rather just let his eyes adjust and trust his instincts.

Reed looked up at the night sky, searching amid the glistening pinholes until he located the North Star, then he shouldered the rifle and stepped into the trees. The owl began to hoot again, and another nocturnal mammal bounded through the leaves. The terrain, littered with rocks and fallen logs, rose and fell beneath him. His body began to warm as he fought his way up the mountainside, hiking toward the ridgeline. The strain and pressure felt good.

"Fight through. Kill or die. Dominate or be a slave. There is no middle ground, Reed."

The top of the ridge burst into view as the trees parted, and Reed knelt behind a boulder, lifting a pair of binoculars to his eyes. The forest that clung to the next ridge was thick, allowing for very little view of what could be hiding amongst it. The cabin sat on the end of the ridge, right at the top of a fifty-yard cliff, while the river cut through the valley in between. It would be impossible to slip down to the water, find a way across, then scale his way to the cabin without being detected. Certainly, there was a method to Oliver's design.

Reed lowered the binoculars and bit his lip. He could position himself on the top of the next ridge and establish a decent overwatch over the cabin, but at seven hundred yards in the dark with all the trees, it was doubtful he would obtain a clear shot. If he approached the cabin from the south along the long and winding driveway that ran along the ridgetop, he would be discovered before he was within half a mile of the mountaintop hideout.

There was really only one option. He would have to run Oliver out of his hole, and there was no subtle way to do it. It was time to launch the fireworks.

11

The top of the next ridge was covered in a dense thicket of evergreens and scrub brush, providing ideal cover as Reed slipped up to the edge and returned the binoculars to his eyes. Two hundred yards below, down a steep hillside covered in rocks and brush, the river wound its way through the ravine. It was about twenty yards wide and surged through the valley floor in a black tide speckled with ice. The far wall of the ravine shot upward in a slope so steep it was almost a cliff. At the top, nestled on the very end of the ridge right before another drop-off, Reed focused the binoculars on the cabin. It sat under the shade of towering pines, built low to the ground out of thick spruce logs. An awning hung off the back, sheltering a green pickup truck and a large stack of firewood. Smoke rose from the chimney, barely visible against the black sky as it drifted into oblivion.

Reed lowered the binoculars and tapped his index finger against them. He'd never seen the cabin before, but he knew the pickup. There were no bumper stickers, scratches, dents, or identifying marks of any kind. It was just a plain Chevy, but he would've recognized it at five hundred yards anywhere in the world. The vehicle was wider than a regular Chevy of that year and sat one inch closer to the ground. That was because of the thick bulletproof plates built into the body beneath the paneling—the daily driver of a kingpin killer.

The cold faded out of Reed's mind as he unslung the backpack and dug into it. He retrieved his Bushnell rangefinder, clicked it on, set the crosshairs over the cabin, and hit the trigger. Oliver's front door sat 367 yards away, at a comparable elevation to Reed's current position. The next item from the backpack was long and dark, consisting of three metal tubes held together by bungee cords. Reed unstrapped them and clicked each one together, then unfolded a metal bipod and locked the tube into it. The weapon was an M224 60mm mortar, and he was well acquainted with its capabilities. Back in Iraq, he'd spent many long hours using identical mortars to shell ISIL entrenchments, and more than a few times, he'd been forced to take cover himself as captured M224s were redirected back at the Marines.

The mortar was heavy, and the metal felt so cold to the touch it almost burned. His fingers stuck to the controls as he adjusted the bipod, squinting through the iron sights as he aimed the weapon toward the cabin. His breath came in short bursts, and his heart rate accelerated with that familiar rush of excitement. Anticipation.

Reed never remembered regretting a kill. From the moment he pressed the trigger on that first contractor in Iraq, to the execution of Oliver's East European thugs at the garbage dump outside of Atlanta. To him, it was all the same. These men deserved to die, for one reason or another, and he was here to prosecute that justice. But tonight, sitting behind the mortar, staring at Oliver's cabin, things felt different. The excitement was a little stronger than the usual rush of anticipation and nervousness. Reed felt eager. Hungry. This was more than an execution—this was a statement. Oliver had broken his own rules, and Reed was going to prosecute him for it.

He checked the elevation of the bipod once more, then reached into the backpack again, more gingerly this time. In the bottom of the pack, carefully wrapped in thick foam padding, were three 60mm mortars. Two were marked with red paint, and the third in a bright green. All three were smooth and clean and glowed in the soft light of the moon with the promise of imminent death just seconds away.

Wind rippled over the top of the ridge, sending leaves cascading over one another in the stillness. The owl started in again, hooting long and slow, as though he knew what was about to happen, and he was mourning the disturbance of his forest retreat. Reed checked the AR-10 and removed the lens caps off the scope before lifting the weapon. He slipped fifty yards down the ridge, ducking under limbs and between the dense shrubbery before stopping in a tiny clearing between two evergreens. He laid the rifle down between the trees, propped up on a stubby bipod, then checked his view of the cabin.

It was perfect. Oliver couldn't possibly escape without exposing himself to Reed's field of fire. The cabin was ideally defensible in that it was impossible to reach without being detected. But in that same way, it was impossible to escape without being cornered. Oliver must have known that. He must have bet on the secrecy of his forest home more than its impregnability.

That's a bet you'll regret for eternity, old man.

Reed left the rifle and retreated back to the mortar, then settled down behind it and lifted the first red shell. It would take a few seconds for the high-explosive round to arc through the air and make contact with the cabin's roof. Within that time, Reed could launch the second shell. The third and final shot would be in the air at the moment the second one detonated. After that, he'd have to run like hell. If Oliver had any unseen defenses in place outside his cabin, Reed's position would be exposed and wide open to them by the time the third round left the tube. His best and only bet would be to move like greased lightning.

Reed set the first shell in the top of the tube, holding it for a moment and feeling its weight and gravity under his fingers. Looking back at the cabin where it lay in silence and stillness, alone at the end of that ridge, it was so quiet and peaceful—a happy place under different circumstances—the kind of place you never wanted to leave.

But not tonight.

Go to hell, old man.

Reed released the shell at the same moment the phone buzzed in his pocket. He jerked his hand back from the tube and lifted the second shell. The first launched with a resounding *whoomp,* flashing through the darkness like a giant spit wad. The second shell launched as the first crashed through the trees and landed on top of the awning. It detonated with a blast so strong the trees over Reed's head swayed, sending dry leaves and dead pine needles showering over his back. The second shell detonated, again sending fire and fury ripping through the log walls as pieces of the pickup truck and shards of shingles rained into the ravine. Reed dropped the final shell into the tube, then dashed for the rifle.

Every part of his body pounded. Foliage exploded in a shower around him as he landed behind the rifle, lifting it and pressing his eye against the scope. The third and final shell landed outside the cabin in a blinding flash of white, sending burning phosphorous showering across the ridgetop and lighting up the area around the cabin as bright as day. The fire burned on, leaving Reed's field of view fully illuminated and at the mercy of his rifle.

The crosshairs of the optic swept over the cabin, first to the rear, then back to the front. The roof of the cabin was blown off, and one wall caved in, now ablaze as greedy flames licked up the dry timber. In moments, the cabin would flood with smoke, and anyone left inside would be forced to flee. The truck also burned, filling the sky with a column of dark black smoke that rose a hundred yards before it began to dissipate. Everything was chaos—the ruined wreckage of two high-explosive rounds and one illumination shell.

Reed flipped off the safety and rested his finger against the trigger while checking the surroundings for any sign of Oliver attempting to flee via a hidden tunnel or a rappelling rope down the cliff. There was nothing but the crackle of the flames and the whistle of the wind as the hideout of the old killer descended into flames. Once more, he swept the crosshairs over the burning wreckage, pausing over every shadow, every possible shelter. There was nothing.

Reed pivoted the scope over the forest, through the flames, and between the trees. Each inhale whistled between his teeth as fresh adrenaline pumped into his blood.

"You son of a bitch. Where are you?"

One more pass of the rifle. The scope was filled with the golden flames and the smog of smoke, reminding him of ancient Catholic paintings of Hell. Everywhere the chaos reigned, but there was no sight of humanity—nobody fleeing the smoke and running for their life into the trees.

The glint of steel caught his eye first: a white flash that reflected the moonlight and contrasted with the blazing orange all around it. He refocused the optic on the spot nestled a hundred feet from the cabin amid the trees. Bushes and shrubs clouded his view, obscuring everything but that hint of steely glow. And then there was a twitch of movement, barely noticeable, but enough to cast a shadow and reveal the full silhouette of the shape.

Oh, shit.

Fire blazed from the trees, filling the scope and blinding him a split second before a whining roar burst across the ravine. Bullets ripped through the trees all around him, shredding limbs and downing saplings in mere seconds. Dirt, rock, and forest debris exploded and rained down on all sides, fogging his vision as the minigun on the opposing ridge continued to rain fire and brimstone on his position.

Reed snatched up his rifle and broke into a run down the ridge, away from the mortar. He ripped his way through the trees and brush, clawing dirt and grime from his face. The ground quaked as small trees toppled down behind him and broken rocks rained down like hail. And still, the gun didn't stop. Hundreds of .30 caliber slugs tore into the ridgetop as the electric gun continued to thunder. Reed's mind began to tunnel on the path ahead, and each step further disoriented his focus.

One thought rang clearly through his panicked mind: *Run like hell.*

A bullet struck the ground inches from his foot, and another sent an explosion of pine bark shooting into his chest like the blast of a shotgun. A limb fell from overhead and struck him in the face. Reed stumbled and almost fell, then burst through a row of evergreens.

By the time he saw the drop-off, there was no prayer of stopping. His left foot gave way first, flying out from under him as he lost hold of the rifle and grabbed at the trees. Sticky green evergreen needles were stripped from the tree as Reed dangled in midair at the edge of the drop-off. Fresh gunfire shredded the evergreens in front of him, and then he fell over the edge and into the darkness below.

12

With perfect clarity, Reed remembered he hadn't purchased rental insurance on the pickup truck.

What a stupid decision.

Then he saw blackness again as he toppled over, free-falling into darkness. For a moment, he couldn't tell if he'd stepped off a cliff or simply overstepped onto a steep slope. The question was answered a second later as his ass collided with the muddy side of a hill. It was steep and wet, leaving nothing for him to grab onto as he rocketed downward. Rocks and sticks tore at his legs and back, and the shadowy silhouettes of trees flashed by on either side. He clawed at thin air, saw the moon, and then he felt the ground vanish beneath him as he left the end of the slope like the end of a water slide and shot into open air.

This time it *was* a cliff, with tall evergreens growing directly beneath him. Reed fell five feet before the first limb struck him in the middle of his lower back. Leaves and branches surrounded him as he crashed through the tops of trees, frantically attempting to grab anything to stop his fall. The blast of the minigun was distant now, drowned out by the pounding of blood in his head. Something tore through his jacket and scraped his ribcage, then a larger limb struck him right in the stomach. The air rushed from his lungs as he clawed at the branch, fighting to hold on. His legs fell, and the limb slipped out of his hands as he went crashing toward the ground until his back collided with the frozen earth.

The wind was ripped from his lungs again, and the sky spun. Reed was vaguely aware of something hot and sticky seeping from his torn jacket. The fear of moments before faded into a blur, along with the vague realization that this was his fault. He had walked straight into a trap.

The minigun stopped firing, and he thought he heard an engine roar to life—a truck, maybe, or an all-terrain vehicle. Tires spun far away, but the sound carried across the empty ravine as clear as though it were right next to his skull.

Reed moved his legs, twisting one at a time to check for functionality. Pain shot through his body, but his legs still worked. Nothing was busted. He grabbed a tree and fought to pull himself into a sitting position, clenching his teeth to fight back a scream. He could feel the tear in his side now, and when he placed his hand over it, fresh blood oozed between his fingers, sticking to his skin. Bits of dirt and sappy needles clung to his jacket and pants, and the dirt further blurred his disoriented vision.

I have to move. He saw me fall.

Reed's legs were stiff as he forced himself to a standing position. Nausea and dizziness racked his brain, but now that he could stand, he managed to focus on a tangible thought to clear his mind.

I'm alive. By some miracle, I'm alive.

He dug out a small LED flashlight from his pocket. It clicked on, but he didn't hear the sound through his ringing ears. One foot forward, then another. The dry leaves rattled against his boots and crunched against the earth. His head still pounded, but thoughts came more clearly now.

My rifle. I need my rifle.

Reed stumbled back toward the base of the cliff and swept the flashlight through the brush. Broken limbs and felled saplings lay everywhere, victims of both his fall and the raking fire of the minigun. He fought his way through the mess and kicked up showers of leaves, but he couldn't see the rifle anywhere. He redirected the light up the thirty-foot cliff to the steep slope above, all the way back up to the top of the ridge.

Damn.

From the moment he'd stepped into thin air Reed had descended almost two-hundred feet, most of it a reckless slide down the muddy slope. He could see his trail between the trees, only narrowly missing mortal collisions with trunks on several occasions.

If the slope had been a cliff, he would be dead now. Hell, if the evergreens at the end of this hellish mudslide hadn't been there and he had free-fallen the last thirty feet, he'd probably be dead. Or have a broken back.

Instead, he was bruised and battered with a few cuts, but nothing fatal.

That's more luck than I can count on.

A thud rang out from behind, jarring Reed from his wonderment. The sound was followed by the roar of an engine. Reed switched the light off and turned back toward the first ridge he had crossed. It was too dark to see, but in the distance, the roar of the motor grew louder, followed by the flash of headlights a hundred yards out, crashing across the forest floor like a tank. He couldn't tell if it was a Jeep or a semitruck, but either way, it was almost on top of him.

Reed broke into a run back through the trees, rushing amid the brush and limbs, away from the ridges, and into the open valley ahead. The river churned on his right, rippling over rocks and gurgling amid the roar of the engine. A gunshot rang out, and the bullet tore through the evergreens, sending yet another shower of sticky needles raining down. Reed dug under his jacket and pried the Glock free, then fired twice. He heard glass shatter, but the engine still roared, almost on his heels. Blood streamed down his side, soaking his jacket and seeping into his pants.

I've got to shake this prick.

Another ten yards of crashing through the brush and a row of giant fir trees loomed up ahead, five yards from the river's edge. Reed dove behind them, rolling to the ground and clawing his way beneath their thick foliage. For the first time, he turned back and peered through the brush at the oncoming vehicle. It was tall, with lights blazing, and big, meaty tires crushing everything in front of it. Definitely not Oliver. The old man had never been one to be this brash or loud. Oliver was more surgical, like Reed. Whoever the hell was driving this thing had no concern for subtlety or discretion. He was here to crush and nothing more.

The Jeep slid to a stop fifty yards away, the big motor rumbling as the dust began to settle around the tires. Reed couldn't see the man inside, but he could see the weapon mounted on the rear bumper of the vehicle. It was the minigun, still piping hot and smoking from the assault of ten minutes before.

He won't leave the Jeep. He can't. Somebody heard the mortars. Cops will be here in another half hour, and he can't afford to be found.

Reed slid the handgun out of his jacket and rested it against the forest floor. The night sights radiated neon green as he aligned the gun with the front tire of the Jeep. A vehicle this big and robust wouldn't be stopped by a single flat tire. It might still limp on, crashing after him, but with two tires down, the party stopped there.

The Glock popped, recoiling in his hand and spitting a 9mm slug fifty yards across the valley floor and directly into the heavy rubber of the tire. The second shot came a moment behind the first. Air hissed from both tires as the engine rumbled, and the driver turned toward the evergreens. Reed jumped up and dashed to the left moments before the front bumper of the vehicle, with two tires flopping against their wheels, hurtled through the fir trees.

By the time the driver realized his mistake, it was much too late to stop. The brakes screamed, but the Jeep hurtled onward, past the trees, across the bank, and nose-first into the river. Water splashed, drowning out the powerful headlights and sending a cascade down over the bank. Reed didn't wait to see what happened next. He turned back through the trees and broke into a run, shielding his face from the whipping branches as he melted into the darkness. In the distance, he heard what he thought sounded like police sirens, but his ears still rang from the explosions and machine-gun fire of the last half hour. Either way, he wasn't waiting to find out what it was.

His lungs and muscles burned, but the running felt good. With each powerful stride, fresh energy and renewed focus filled his mind. He could hear the sirens for sure now, coming from the south, rising and falling as the police drew closer. Another few minutes, and they would be at the cabin.

Reed stopped at the base of the cliff and peered upward, back to the place he had fallen from minutes before—a full hundred feet up a sheer wall of mud and rock. There was no way he could fight his way back to the top, and even if he somehow managed the impossible, the police would quickly blanket the woods before he could sneak the three miles back to the pickup.

He turned to the west and resumed jogging through the forest. His muscles ached and his right side burned like hell, but he blocked it all out, pounding onward.

Miles passed under his boots before he broke out of the trees and onto a narrow gravel road that he remembered from studying maps of Oliver's cabin area. There was a hunting camp another few miles away, and with luck, there would be a vehicle he could hot-wire and use to get back on the road.

All of his gear was back in the truck. After the police cleared out, he would return to recover his weapons and work on a new plan. For now, he needed to get as far away from the mad killer as possible and figure out where the hell Oliver disappeared to.

13

Western North Carolina

Reed drove north out of Cherokee and into Graham County. The sun broke over the horizon, draping the rural mountain roads in a warm glow that reflected off the frosty tree limbs. In the tiny town of Robbinsville, the old truck squeaked like a rusty tractor as it rolled to a stop. It was a Ford, maybe a mid-seventies model, with rotten floorboards and a cracked windshield. A few years' worth of mud and grime clung to the body panels, covering the faded bumper stickers and empty soda bottles. The power steering was gone, and the alignment was way out, making it a constant battle to keep the battered vehicle on the road. But the truck ran, and at this point, that was all he could ask for.

Still better than walking.

At a gas station, the engine died as Reed pulled the ignition wires apart. His head ached. His body ached.

The muscles in his toes ached. The injuries from the chaos in Atlanta were far from healed, and the bitter wind that swept through the open floorboard of the truck served to numb the skin and make every part of him stiffen. Add to that the injuries and battering of the night before, and he felt about as worn and creaky as his ride.

He dug through his pockets and found the bottle of heavy-duty pain killers that Kelly left him. The pills tasted bitter as they rolled over his tongue, and he swallowed them dry. He was reluctant to dull his mind with an opioid, but at this stage, the surging pain was a greater threat to his focus.

In a few moments, he took a mental inventory of what gear he had left on his person. It wasn't much—most of his essential equipment had been in the backpack, and everything else was in the truck. The only things he had on him were a knife, the Glock, a few magazines, a flashlight, a fake South Carolina driver's license, sixty bucks, a lighter, and half a dozen cigarettes—hardly the stuff of a war-ready killer. Not even any communication.

Wait.

Reed suddenly remembered his phone in the interior pocket of his jacket. The phone had vibrated right before he launched the first mortar, but at the time, he hadn't given it a second thought. Now the reality rang clear in his tired mind: His phone vibrated only for a few critical contacts.

When he unlocked it, the first notification he got was for a low battery. He dismissed the warning and navigated to the single text message. It was from Oliver.

NICE TRY REED. ENJOY THE WOLF.

Reed cursed and slammed his hand into the steering wheel. He started to reply to the message, but the phone's screen went black, and the "*charge battery*" symbol flashed.

Shit!

Reed had been a fool to assault the cabin so brashly. It was a rookie move—the kind that belonged in open warfare, not the art of assassination. He wasn't even sure whether Oliver was in the cabin at all, yet he had shelled that place and lit it up like a damn fireworks show.

I didn't care if he was there. I wanted to make a statement. I wanted to shit on his porch the way he shit on mine. Such a fool.

He drummed his finger on the wheel and stared out the window.

Who is The Wolf? The man in the Jeep?

Reed had never heard of a killer named *The Wolf*. All of Oliver's contractors had nicknames or call signs. Reed's was *Prosecutor,* and he knew every other killer by theirs. The Wolf wasn't on the list. It had to be somebody external to the company. Somebody willing to kill another contractor.

The next thought that rang through his tired mind was more chilling: *Oliver wouldn't hire somebody outside of his own company.* It was contrary to the old man's standards of operation. He didn't trust people he didn't control, and even though Oliver would be reluctant to set one of his own killers against a fellow contractor, it might be better than letting loose a rampaging madman with a minigun.

But Oliver *had* unleashed a madman with a minigun, which could only mean one of two things: Either Oliver had lost his mind, or he was no longer calling the shots. Reed remembered the contract for Mitchell Holiday, a state senator for Georgia he had been hired to kill right before Oliver turned on him. Who wanted Holiday dead? It was a question he had never been able to answer, and now it seemed more pivotal to this entire mess than ever. Somebody bigger than Oliver wanted Holiday dead, and now they wanted Reed dead.

Reed closed his eyes and thought back to his last encounter with Oliver—at Pratt Pullman Yard, in east Atlanta. It was there that Oliver admitted to his dastardly scheme to send Reed back to prison, there to be murdered in his sleep, removing him from Oliver's list of outstanding liabilities and loose ends. But Oliver wasn't the one who ordered the Holiday hit. No, Oliver had said the job was legitimate, ordered by the men Salvador worked for.

Salvador. The shady South American who had stood beside Oliver at Pratt Pullman. It was Salvador who hired the goons that Reed killed in Atlanta. Salvador who kidnapped Banks, and represented the interests of the people who wanted Holiday dead. Salvador, not Oliver, was the link to these people— these people who would stop at nothing to destroy Holiday, and now Reed.

And I don't know who they are. That thought was the

most terrifying of all. Reed could take on a battalion of Army Rangers if he had to, as long as he knew more about them than they knew about him. Information was his greatest asset, and right now, he had none.

Reed shook his head to clear it.

Time to get moving. This prick will be back.

He dug through the glove box, dumping the contents onto the passenger seat. There was a vehicle registration, a box of replacement fuses, and a folded map of the tristate area. Nothing else.

He pocketed the map, then slammed the box shut and stepped out of the truck, kicking the mud off his boots as he went. He glanced around the small service station and noticed a couple locals watching him from adjacent pumps. He wasn't sure if it was his angry body language or the rattletrap truck that was drawing more attention.

The clerk inside the store appeared much less inquisitive. He stared through the window with a dazed look, as though his mind were a thousand miles away in another universe. Reed picked up a bottle of water and walked to the counter, dropping a twenty-dollar bill onto it.

"Ten on three. And can I get some quarters?"

The attendant accepted the money and handed Reed his change. Reed cracked the water bottle open and took a swig as he walked back to the truck. He put ten dollars into the almost empty tank, then drove across the street to a Dollar General. A narrow metal roof sheltered a payphone next to the store. He dropped two quarters in, then dialed the phone.

"Lasquo Financial. How may I direct your call?"

Lasquo financial was the banking headquarters for the criminal underworld. Reed held most of his assets and loose cash with them and enjoyed the luxury of conducting business anywhere in the world with a quick phone call. After repeating his memorized series of coded phrases, he asked for Thomas Lancaster. The phone went silent for a moment, then the familiar New Orleans drawl of Reed's personal banker rang over the phone.

"Reed, good to hear from you. What can I do for you?"

"I need you to send me a couple grand by Western Union to the Dollar General in Robbinsville, North Carolina."

"Right away. Anything else?"

"No, that's everything. Thank you."

Reed hung up and dropped two more quarters into the phone. It rang twice.

"Winter."

If Lasquo was the criminal world's banking institution, Winter was its eye in the sky. A nameless, genderless, faceless entity on the other side of the phone who answered questions that needed to be answered, found people who needed to be found and dealt with information as a commodity. Reed had called Winter before when things went south in Atlanta, and Winter had been uncharacteristically unhelpful. This time, Reed wouldn't take silence for an answer.

"No bullshit, Winter. Where is Oliver?"

The phone was silent.

Reed wrapped his fingers around the metal roof over the phone. His knuckles turned white. "I know you know. You've been in on this shit from the start. Now you better start talking or—"

"You would be prudent not to threaten me, Reed." It was the first time Reed had ever heard emotion from the ghost on the other end of the line. "I'm not your ally. Don't make me your enemy."

Reed slammed his fist into the wall of the store but didn't snap back. "All right. Fine. So, I'm going to ask you some questions, and you're going to find the answers. That's what you do, right?"

"That depends on the question."

"How about this? Who ordered the hit on Mitch Holiday?"

The phone was silent. Reed gritted his teeth again and waited. Finally, Winter answered. The voice was soft, and Reed almost thought he heard fear in the tone.

"I don't know."

"*What?*"

"I launched an inquiry. My sources are . . . unhelpful."

"Okay, so where's Oliver?"

"I don't know."

Reed shook his head. "No, that's not how you work. You always know, remember? Now I just burned Oliver's cabin to the ground, and he's not there."

"Good for you." Winter sounded almost sarcastic. "I don't know where he is."

"Okay, then tell me something you *do know*."

"I know that if I were you, I'd stop asking questions and get lost while I still had the chance. I've been around for a long time, Reed. Long enough to know when something smells like death."

"That's not good enough!" Reed snapped. He waited, but the phone didn't cut off. Reed relaxed his clenched fist. "Just point me in the right direction. I've always taken care of you. You know I'm the real deal. Cut me some slack, and I'll cut you loose."

Winter's methodical breathing hissed over the phone, and Reed waited patiently against the phone booth.

"I know somebody is behind this," he said. "Somebody bigger than Oliver."

"Yes."

"They want me dead. They want Mitch Holiday dead."

"They do."

"So, who are they?"

Now Reed couldn't even hear Winter's breaths.

"Watch your back, Reed. Don't call me again." The line went dead.

Reed cursed and slammed the handset back onto the receiver. He spat on the sidewalk and walked inside the Dollar General, where the Western Union wire waited for him. Two grand, sent from a shell company out of Arkansas. Reed accepted the cash, then walked back to the truck and got in, rubbing the folded bills between his fingers as he watched the passing traffic.

There's a bounty on my head. This Wolf guy was hired especially for me.

Without knowing who was after him, there was little Reed could do besides run and be reactionary. He didn't know this man, and he didn't know his tactics, although it was obvious he had a flair for the dramatic. That was certainly outside the realm of Oliver's contractors, who would always prefer a knife to the throat over a minigun mounted on a Jeep. The Wolf was different. He was brash. Unpredictable.

Reed tapped his finger on his knee and looked up the highway. The temperature had dropped another few degrees. An occasional snowflake drifted past the cab, landing on the ground and fading into the concrete. Even though it was hardly midmorning, there was already a small crowd of bustling locals moving in and out of the gas station and the local diner. It was fifty miles back to Oliver's cabin—plenty of space to buy Reed a little time before he could expect The Wolf to come sniffing around.

He rubbed the exhaustion out of his eyes and started the truck. Half a mile down the road, he found a small grocery store with an empty lot behind it. He parked the truck next to a dumpster and double-checked to make sure the doors were locked, and then he lay across the bench seat. He would sleep for a couple hours, refresh his mind, and reset his battered body. Then he would regroup and resume his hunt for the kingpin killer.

Reed's eyes snapped open as though prompted by a gunshot. Even before he sat up, he knew he had slept much longer than he intended. A glance at his watch confirmed what he already feared: It was four p.m.

Shit.

It was the drugs. It had to be. He never slept that hard, especially under these circumstances. Sitting up, Reed blinked back the fog of sleep and scooped up the bottle from the convenience store. The icy water cooled his dry throat, and he drained it before taking a quick glance around the pickup. From his position next to the dumpster, Reed could see half of the main intersection, along with a good portion of the grocery store's parking lot. A couple women walked next to each other toward the store, while a single man in a blue jacket hurried toward his car with a bag of groceries. The sky, once bright with sunlight, was now blanketed by dark grey clouds, and flecks of snow drifted through the air and landed on the hood of the truck. Reed couldn't tell for sure, but the wind that whispered through the cracks in the floorboard felt colder than before. The temperature was still dropping.

He reached for his phone then remembered that it was dead. That left him with nothing but a handful of quarters and a single payphone, but there wasn't really anyone to call. Without Winter, finding Oliver would be next to impossible. He hoped to get lucky back at the cabin, but that turned out to be a trap from the start. Oliver must have anticipated his arrival. He probably wasn't even in the country.

Reed's thoughts were broken off by the sight of a

silver Mercedes with jet-black windows—definitely a coupe, but as big as a sedan, not more than a year old, with gleaming trim and wide black tires. It rolled gracefully down the street, well under the speed limit, sticking out like a sore thumb amid the battered SUVs and rusted pickups.

Nobody in a town like this drove a car like that. Reed sank back in the seat and laid his hand on the Glock. The pickup was fully exposed to the view of the Mercedes, and Reed felt suddenly vulnerable and wanted to jump out, but he sank deeper into the seat and waited.

The Mercedes rolled up to the intersection, thirty yards down the street. It stopped at the sign, its nose pointed directly at the side of the pickup. A cloud of grey vapor built behind the rear bumper, rising toward the sky as the car idled. Reed could see the man behind the wheel now. He was trim and fit, clean-shaven, with short black hair, sitting with one hand on the wheel at the twelve o'clock position, and the other out of sight beneath the dash. In the dying light, Reed could make out the veins in his neck, bulging and contracting with each breath. The quiet, collected calm of his features mixed with his narrow, darting eyes.

It was The Wolf. Reed knew it without ever having seen him before. The cold in his eyes, and hard lines of his face told the story better than Winter ever could.

The reality hit him just as the black eyes twitched to the right and locked with his. For a moment, the man in the Mercedes stared at him without blinking, and then a tight smirk spread across his lips.

Reed's hands darted to the ignition wires. The sharp copper dug into his fingers as he separated the red from the black, the blue from the yellow. The bite of wire in trembling skin hadn't changed over the past ten years since he hotwired his first car back in Orange County. He remembered the sweat that puddled in his palms as he fought with each wire, trying to ignore the frantic badgering of his stressed-out accomplice from Oakland. Even months later, after dozens of stolen cars, his fingers still shook. Over time, the tremors that ran down his arms felt less like fear and more like excitement.

But not now. Now those tremors felt like nerves that might well cost him his life.

Reed rubbed two exposed copper tips against each other, and a loud click rang out from beneath the floorboard, but the motor didn't turn. A fresh shiver racked his arms, and he fumbled to pick up a dropped wire, then pressed them together again—another click, and then silence.

Run.

The big motor of the Mercedes rumbled from the intersection. Reed kicked the door open and flung himself out, making a quick dash for the shelter of the alley behind the grocery store. He remembered the night before—the thunder of the minigun as brush and trees crashed to the earth—fire, hot lead, and total chaos. This man was insane, whoever he was. A complete maniac. Allowing a repeat of that performance in the tight confines of this small town would result in a bloodbath of innocent civilians, and Reed couldn't live with that. He imagined the avalanche of bullets blasting holes through the Wendy's across the street or tearing through the Family Dollar straight ahead. He wouldn't allow The Wolf to go to war in this place. Reed would lose him first, then find his way outside of Robbinsville to a more isolated locale— someplace he could ambush and kill this rabid dog without needless death.

Reed jogged across the street, leaving the shelter of the alley and huddling close to the front wall of the Family Dollar. Locals bustled back and forth between SUVs and minivans, their shoes knocking against the frozen pavement. He felt the comforting hard plastic of the Glock beneath his jacket and tossed another glance around the parking lot for the Mercedes. It was nowhere in sight.

Come on, you bastard. Take it out of town.

Drops of sleet flashed past his face. Somebody honked, and a child cried. Reed ducked behind a pickup truck and turned away from the store. A mother herded her screaming toddler toward her Honda and shot Reed a suspicious glare as he stumbled past her, his gaze still sweeping the streets.

He started back toward the main road, and then he saw it. Black on silver, purring down the street only fifty yards away, with the giant Mercedes logo glowing in the middle of the front grill. A split-second passed, then the Mercedes coughed, and the back tires spun. Reed stepped away from the mother and child and wrapped his fingers around the pistol.

"Chris?"

14

The voice sent a shockwave ripping through Reed's body. He twisted on his heel, back toward the store. She stood outside the Family Dollar, bundled in a thick red jacket with a snow-white knit cap pulled down low over her golden hair. Her cheeks were rosy red in the bite of the wind, and her eyes, once as bright blue as the Gulf of Mexico, were now frozen sapphires, shining just as bright and beautiful.

Banks.

Reed's mind shut down, and the world around him ceased to exist as he stared at her. The curve of her body beneath the jacket. Her delicate fingers curled around a plastic shopping bag loaded with groceries. She was as perfect as the first moment he met her, and in a flash, his mind was ripped back to Atlanta. Back to the hospital hallway where he looked her in the eyes and said goodbye. The hardest thing he'd ever done. Walking away from a woman he cared for—cared for so deeply he didn't believe it could be real.

Her eyes broke right through his carefully orches-
trated detachment and sank into his soul. In an instant,
all the confused emotions of the past few days returned
—the longing, self-doubt, obsessive affection. It took all
the willpower he'd ever mustered to walk away from
her three days before in that hospital. And here she
was, in the middle of this isolated little town, with a
killer just around the corner.

"Chris . . . what are you doing here?"

The words had barely left her lips before Reed
heard the snarl of the Mercedes, now only yards away.
The car was rocketing through the intersection and
roaring toward them. There could be no mistake now.
The driver was here for him.

"Get down!" Reed lunged forward and grabbed
Banks, pulling her with him behind the nearest SUV. A
second later, gunshots rang out across the parking lot.
Reed recognized the chattering snarl immediately—
rapid shots stacked on top of each other in a constant
spray of lead. It was an Uzi—short-barreled, nine-
millimeter. Not the glovebox gun of your average North
Carolina redneck.

More gunfire roared from across the parking lot,
and glass shattered from the rear of the SUV, pelting
down over their heads in tiny black cubes. Reed pulled
Banks lower and jerked the pistol from beneath his
jacket. Twisting around the end of the SUV, he pointed
it in the general direction of the Mercedes and fired
twice. Another blast from the open window of the
coupe sent a storm of bullets slamming into the rear
hatch of the SUV and skipping against the ground.

Reed's infuriation grew with every twisting ache in his stomach. He grabbed Banks by the arm and jerked his head toward the far end of the parking lot. "Get up! Run!"

Banks's shoulders trembled, but she shook her head. "No! This way. I've got my car!"

Before Reed could stop her, Banks jumped to her feet and ran around the front of the SUV. He scrambled to follow her, weaving between the parked vehicles as the Mercedes roared again. Banks's bright yellow Super Beetle was hidden between two pickup trucks at the back of the lot, a dusting of snow building on its roof. Banks stood by the door, fumbling with her keys, when they slipped out of her hands and hit the concrete. She cursed and picked them up, dropping the groceries.

Reed snatched the keys from her hand and jerked the door open. "Climb in!"

"My snacks!" Banks objected.

"*Leave them.* Get in!"

He shoved Banks through the door and piled in after her, smacking his head against the low roofline of the car. He shoved the keys into the ignition and pressed the clutch against the floor, remembering the last time he and Banks had taken a drive in the vintage German car. The Beetle hadn't started; he prayed this time it would.

The motor turned over with a low whine, then coughed to life. Reed's knees were crowded against the dashboard, spread out on either side of the steering wheel, with barely an inch to spare. The Mercedes snarled from someplace behind, and he slammed the

Beetle into first gear before planting his foot into the accelerator.

The rear tires of the little car squealed and spun on the frozen pavement. Reed swung the wheel to the right, and the Beetle shot forward, sliding between parked pickup trucks and into the parking lot. Another string of automatic gunfire ripped between the trucks, and bullets smacked the rear hatch of the Beetle, shattering the back glass.

Banks screamed, "Oscar!"

Reed jerked the wheel back to the left and turned the car toward the street. Lost behind them, the Mercedes was caught amid the tangle of bigger vehicles, and the mountain walls echoed with the clatter of the Uzi and the desperate whine of the undersized Volkswagen engine. Reed shifted into second gear and launched the Beetle onto the street. The front windshield was all but obscured by frost and fog, and Reed squinted through it, shifting into third gear as the speedometer passed forty miles per hour.

"Clear the windshield! I can't see!"

Banks leaned forward, jerking her hat off and pawing at the glass. Her hair exploded in a cloud of static, obscuring his vision as he fought to see through the fog. She sat back, leaving a cleaned section of windshield about the size of a dinner plate.

"Dog!" Banks shouted.

Reed jerked the wheel to the left just in time to miss a Labrador standing in the middle of his lane. Houses flashed past, and he swerved back to the right as a school bus blasted by them, blaring its horn.

Small stores and restaurants rocketed by on both sides.

A street sign read State Hwy 129. Reed looked into the diminutive rearview mirror and caught sight of the Mercedes a couple hundred yards behind. Gears shrieked and groaned as Reed shifted into fourth and pressed the gas pedal to the floor. The motor strained, and the speedometer bounced at the sixty-five mark.

"Doesn't this thing go any faster?"

"He's old!" Banks shouted. "Don't yell at him!"

Reed swung the little car into a wide turn and downshifted. The tachometer rocketed up to the red line, and the motor whined like it was about to explode. Above it all, Reed heard the thunder of the big Mercedes, and the silver sedan closed the ground behind them in mere seconds. He could see the silhouette of the driver now: tall, lean, staring straight ahead with that same smirk plastered to his lips.

"Get down!"

Reed grabbed Banks by the neck and shoved her forward. He saw the muzzle of the Uzi pass through the open window of the Mercedes, and orange fire blazed through the twilight. Bullets zipped toward the Beetle and crashed through the thin metal. The windshield shattered as Reed jerked the car to the left into the oncoming lane. The Mercedes followed behind him, and Reed pulled back to the right. Once more, the big coupe swerved to follow. More gunshots rattled in his ear, and the rearview mirror affixed to the driver's door exploded and vanished as 9mm slugs tore into it. Reed slammed the Beetle back into fourth gear and jammed his leg so hard into the accelerator he thought he might punch straight through the floorboard. The car strained and gained a couple miles per hour, but it wasn't enough. He would never outrun a modern performance car. The killer behind him in the coupe would shoot him or run him off the road long before Reed could hope to lose him.

Banks spat hair out of her mouth and sat up, looking through the shattered rear glass. "Gun!" she shouted, and grabbed the wheel, jerking it to the left.

The Beetle swung back into the oncoming lane just as another burst of automatic gunfire shredded the air behind them. The driver of a pickup truck twenty yards ahead laid on its horn. Reed shoved Banks away from the wheel and pulled back to the right, swerving out of the way of the oncoming truck with milliseconds to spare.

"Chris!" Banks screamed. "What the *hell* is going on?"

Reed's mind raced, and he looked out the window to the right. A steep hill rose directly from the shoulder of the lane, with metal mesh staked into the frozen dirt to keep falling rocks off the road. To his left, the hillside dropped off into a short cliff, followed by another narrow ledge. Straight ahead, the highway continued, weaving its way into the mountains and toward Tennessee. A single sign protruded from the frozen earth:

DEALS GAP MOTORCYCLE RESORT — 1 MILE.

Reed had been there before. The previous summer, with his Camaro. He drove his car into these mountains as part of a charity cruise, just past the motorcycle resort, right on the state line.

"Buckle in!" he shouted, then swerved to the left as another string of gunfire roared from behind.

The Beetle topped a slight rise in the road, and Reed swerved into the left lane before stomping on the brakes. The little car's tires screamed on the pavement, and the Beetle slid twenty yards down the far side of the hill. The Mercedes flashed past on his right and continued down the hill before the driver could apply the brakes.

Reed planted his foot into the gas pedal again and continued down the hill a hundred yards before turning sharply to the left at an intersection. The new road was two lanes wide, with wide yellow stripes down the middle. Reed heard the Mercedes roaring back up the hill behind him as he worked his way through the gears. The Beetle groaned and squeaked at every bump, and what was left of the windshield was covered in frost, but Reed could now see through the shattered hole in the middle.

Banks clicked her seatbelt into place and watched through the rear glass, her eyes wide with fear. "He's coming, Chris. He's coming back."

Reed looked into the rearview mirror once, then ahead. The road curved to the right, then back to the left, and another intersection flashed by. The motor-cycle resort sat between the trees where two roads intersected, and fifty yards past the resort, a yellow sign mounted on a metal pole stood beside the road.

WARNING: TAIL OF THE DRAGON PASS. 318 CURVES NEXT 11 MILES.

Memories from the previous summer came rushing back. Hairpin turns wrapping around empty drop-offs, often without so much as a guardrail for protection. Car clubs from all across America traveled annually to ride the famous Tail, testing their curving performance against one of the most challenging natural tracks on the East Coast. But that was during the summer—never during the winter. Never with ice on the road. The pile of scrapped cars was high enough when the pavement was hot and sticky—racing the Tail during the winter was a death wish.

Reed shifted into fourth and pressed the pedal to the floor. Just this once, daring the Tail in winter seemed the safer option.

Banks saw the sign and then shook her head as she reached for the steering wheel. "No, no, Chris! What are you doing?"

"I can't outrun him," Reed shouted over the roar of the wind. "I'm gonna have to out-drive him."

The first turn snapped back to the left out of nowhere, completing almost 180 degrees as the road dove downward. Reed relaxed on the gas and pulled the parking brake. The rear wheels locked and screamed, and the tail of the car pivoted outward as a rock wall passed directly in front of them. Banks screamed. The car rolled to the right. Reed slammed his shoulder into the door, shifting his weight back to the left as he released the brake and stomped on the gas again. The car swung out of the turn with another screech of tires, and Reed spun the wheel to the right just in time to slide into the next curve. In the rearview mirror, he caught sight of the Mercedes laying on its brakes. The bigger car slid and fishtailed as the driver struggled to reduce his speed without flying off the road. The distance between The Wolf and his prey was increasing as Reed powered into the next curve.

The Beetle was no drift car. It had barely enough power to break each slide, and the suspension was too loose and too high to control the body roll. With every turn, the car swung wildly to the outside of the curve, and he imagined the wheels lifting off the ground. The only saving grace were relatively new tires that gripped the pavement well enough to overcome some of the loose suspension.

"Grab the dash!" Reed shouted. "When I say, lean toward me."

He downshifted and dumped the clutch. The motor howled as though it were about to burst. Reed planted his foot against the brake and swung the wheel to the right as the next hairpin curve enveloped them.

"Now!"

Banks leaned against him, and Reed pressed his weight against the left window as the car slid around another curve. The rear bumper swung out, and this time Reed was certain the driver's side wheels left the ground. The car tipped and hopped, and Reed slung his weight into the door. The tires hit the ground again, and the stench of burnt rubber filled the cabin. A blast of bitter wind ripped through the shattered rear glass, and Reed couldn't help but feel a bolt of lightning streak through his veins.

This was it. Even here, in a race for his life, this was the thrill that kept him coming back for more. The addiction of too much speed and not enough safety. It was what made him love the Camaro, love the chase, and love pushing himself to the limit. Because in this moment, The Wolf didn't matter. His confused feelings for Banks were less overwhelming. Only the thin line between himself and certain death held his attention as he danced down it, one hairpin curve after another.

In the rearview mirror, the Mercedes had fallen back a full hundred yards, struggling around a curve in the road. The big car struggled to make the tight turns, and the back tires were sliding off the road, slinging dirt and leaves in a cascade of brown.

Rejuvenated by his inevitable triumph, Reed smacked the steering wheel. "I've got you now, bitch."

"Congratulations!" Banks snapped. "Now, slow the hell down and get us out of here!"

Two more curves flashed past the car, and Reed alternated leaning into his door and leaning toward Banks, keeping the car planted on the pavement. White flecks of snow appeared on the frozen asphalt, sparse at first, but starting to thicken. The sky boiled with grey clouds, and the inside of the car felt like the interior of a deep freezer.

"Chris! Slow down. He's gone now."

Reed couldn't see the Mercedes, but he knew the driver wasn't far behind. He needed to put at least a mile of distance between them before the road ended. That would give him maybe ninety seconds to find a place to hide the Volkswagen and take cover.

Reed relaxed off the gas a little and screeched into another curve. The mountains rose on either side of the road in steep, tree-covered slopes, with the occasional ravine in between. He couldn't see more than fifty yards ahead through the curves. Large flakes glided off the hood of the car and gathered against the base of the windshield, perfectly white against the dirty yellow. The wind whistled and beat against the loose windows, making every part of the car rattle as they started down a hill.

"He won't be far behind," Reed muttered. "Once we get through the pass, we've got to ditch the car."

"Why is he shooting at you?" Banks still gripped the dash, her fingers the same color as her pale cheeks. In spite of the cold, beads of sweat gathered on her forehead, and her upper lip trembled.

Reed felt no fear. His hands were steady as he gripped the wheel with his left and rested his right against the gear shifter. Nothing about death scared him, but her eyes, so clear and enchanting—the fear and strain he saw was overwhelming; it pierced him to his core, making his stomach twist and his mind go blank. As the thrill of the run began to fade, the longing in his heart returned. All he wanted to do was hold her.

"Watch the road!"

A turn loomed ahead, veering sharply to the left as a steep hillside rose up directly beyond. Reed jerked the car out of gear and slammed his foot against the brake. Something snapped, as sharp and loud as a gunshot. The brake pedal went limp, and Reed's chest tightened. He snatched the emergency brake. The rear tires locked and screeched as the Beetle began to fish-tail. Reed struggled to direct the car around the turn, but the back end swung out too far. Banks's mouth hung open, but no sound came out as her nails dug into his forearm.

Panic dulled his finer senses. The windows turned black in a storm of dirt as the air filled with Banks's screams. In what felt like slow motion, he reached out and grabbed her hand. The car lurched over an obstruction in the ditch and hurtled forward as their eyes met, building what might be the last memory he'd ever make.

I love her.

15

Tennessee/North Carolina State Line

The rear bumper of the Beetle dug into the hillside, and Reed's head slammed against the steering wheel as metal and glass crunched all around him. The engine hatch buckled in the rear of the car, sending a wave of heat flooding through the busted rear window. Reed coughed and clawed at his eyes as he spilled out of the VW and into the snow. The forest around him danced as though the ground were a magic carpet, rippling with every blast of the frozen wind.

Banks. Where's Banks?

He stumbled back to the car, still swaying on his feet, and reached through the mangled doorframe, fishing for her arm. Banks moved and coughed, and his fingers found her shoulder.

"Can you hear me? Are you okay?"

"You wrecked my car, you deadbeat!"

The muscles in his chest loosened at her emotional

outburst. At least she was alive. Reed staggered into the ditch, the world around him wavering as he leaned against the smashed car. Tree limbs danced and swayed overhead, furthering his disorientation as he took stock of his surroundings.

The Beetle was done. One tire was blown, the back hatch had buckled as it collided with a boulder, and oil streamed over the clay. The frame must have twisted on impact—the entire car was warped, and both windows were shattered.

Reed stumbled around the front bumper and jerked on the passenger's door. It took him a moment to pry it open, but when he did, Banks fell out, coughing and rubbing her eyes. The cold sweat glistening on her face was already freezing under the sting of the wind.

Reed grabbed her by the hand and motioned at the hillside. "Come on! We've got to go."

They fought their way up the hill, using trees and fallen logs to help pull themselves up the slope. Banks coughed and fought her way up behind him, slipping on rock-hard clay. In the distance, a roar echoed through the mountains. He wasn't sure if it was the voice of the wind or the snarl of the Mercedes. Either way, they didn't have much time.

A fallen log lay halfway up the hill where the slope moderated and opened up onto a narrow plateau running along the side of the mountain. Farther on, the hillside became a rocky cliff face and shot skyward another forty yards, with trees growing out of the rock.

The spray of snow raining from the sky had become a shower, larger flakes falling closer together and obscuring his view. The leaves were speckled white now, with fading patches of brown. Reed stopped just past the log and panted, glancing back toward the Beetle. They had cleared a hundred yards up the hill, leaving the road a winding grey snake, rapidly turning white.

The Mercedes roared.

"Get down!"

Banks gasped as he grabbed her, and they crashed to the ground behind the log. New frustration clouded his mind as their situation unfolded. For the moment, they were hidden, but there was no egress off of this hill without exposing themselves.

He held her trembling fingers between his and nodded. "Stay quiet. It's going to be okay."

Moments slipped by. Reed heard the Mercedes rumble around the turns and then glide to a halt at the bottom of the hill. Propping himself up on his elbows, Reed crawled to the right as his heart thumped like a drum.

"What is it?" Banks whispered.

Reed held his finger to his lips and peered around the end of the log. The tinted windows of the Mercedes at the bottom of the hill were too dark to see through in the gathering darkness. Snow melted and streamed off the silver hood under the heat of the big motor, while exhaust billowed from the rear bumper. After almost a minute, the driver's door opened, and a slender white male stepped out. He was maybe five-ten, with skinny arms, holding what looked to be a glass Coke bottle in his right hand. He set the bottle on the roof of the car and stretched, rolling his neck to either side. The Wolf wore black slacks with shiny dress shoes. His torso was wrapped in a thick peacoat, but beneath the V of the collar, Reed could make out a suit jacket and a dark blue tie. The man's hair was close-cropped, almost shaved on the sides, and just long enough on top to comb over. He wore dark, aviator-style sunglasses, and black leather gloves.

Gloves. Who the hell wears gloves while driving?

Banks lay on the ground with her elbows dug into the leaves, biting her lower lip as she peered over the top of the log.

Reed shook his head and pulled on her sleeve. "*Get down.*"

Banks glared at him and swatted his hand away. Reed heard a crunching sound at the bottom of the hill and turned to see the man stepping gingerly through the snow toward the Beetle. He walked as if he were crossing a frozen lake—as if each step might break the ice—and he set each foot against the ground, feeling out the clay before placing his weight on it. He approached the Volkswagen from the rear and peered into the shattered glass, then walked back to the driver's side of the Mercedes, high-stepping the whole way.

Bent over, he gazed into the rearview mirror, brushing snow off his coat before adjusting his tie with a careful twist of both hands. He straightened, then adjusted his sunglasses as he walked to the rear of the car and swept his foot beneath the bumper. The lid of the trunk popped open automatically, and he dug inside for a moment.

Reed reached beneath his jacket and checked for his pistol. It was still there, only half-loaded now. He couldn't guarantee a lethal shot at a hundred yards. It was just too far. He might miss or hit an inessential body part, and then they'd be exposed and still short on firepower.

The Wolf emerged from the trunk with a long black case in his hands. He set it on the ground and snapped it open, then withdrew a black rifle-style weapon with a thick barrel and a wide drum mounted beneath the receiver. Reed squinted and tilted his head for a better view, watching as The Wolf pulled the charging handle on the side of the weapon.

"What the hell is that?" Banks hissed.

The Wolf lifted the Coke off the roof of the car, took a long swig, and then adjusted his sunglasses again. He set the bottle back down and raised the weapon into his shoulder, directing it into the trees.

Oh, shit.

A *shoonk* echoed from the roadway, followed by a brief pause, as something grey and golfball-sized arced through the air and thudded into the hillside to Reed's left. A deafening blast shook the mountainside, and snow and forest debris exploded over the hill amid a cloud of smoke.

Shoonk, shoonk, shoonk!

Banks jumped to her feet and dashed into the trees, shouting at Reed to follow. More explosions detonated against the hillside, throwing sticks and rocks around him as Reed fought to catch up with her. The grenade launcher continued to fire from the roadbed below, and each blast fell a little closer to home. Something sharp and hard tore through his pants and bit into his leg, and one more explosion blasted from above, sending a torrent of rocks crashing down over their heads.

"Banks! Get down!"

Reed slid to a stop behind a tree, Banks only feet away behind another trunk. He looked down the hillside and made eye contact with the black-clothed killer. That dancing smirk returned beneath flushed cheeks as The Wolf fed fresh grenades into the drum of the launcher.

Shoonk!

Another grenade exploded only a few yards away.

Banks shouted, then tumbled through the brush and crashed to the ground beside him. "Give me the gun! I'll cap that son of a bitch!" Her eyes were consumed by wildfire.

She's crazy.

Shoonk! Shoonk!

"Run!" Reed wrapped his fingers around hers, and they took off into the trees, running along the plateau. The slope beneath them was still gentle, but the frozen ground was slick, and they struggled to find footing as they crashed between the trees. The snowfall thickened as grenades detonated behind them, but the killer's aim was obstructed by the forest. Footsteps pounded behind them, and then they heard a fresh noise—the hissing, popping snarl of a suppressed assault weapon. Bullets ripped through the undergrowth around them.

"Who *is* this guy?" Banks screamed.

Reed ducked behind a tree as a string of bullets

ripped over his shoulder. He pointed the Glock back toward the shooter and pulled the trigger. The gun clicked over a bad primer and didn't fire. Another roar of gunfire shredded branches and rained bark over their heads as Reed pulled back behind the tree.

"Here. Give it to me!" Banks jerked the gun out of his hand before he could stop her, and with a quick twist of her wrist, she ejected the bad cartridge and pumped a new one into the chamber. She moved as though she were on skates and slid out from behind the tree, then raised the gun. The Glock barked, spitting hot lead through the trees, and a shout broke out from far behind them. The assault rifle fell silent.

Reed stared as Banks lowered the gun and turned back to him, her eyes blazing with vicious fire. "What?" She tossed him the gun. "Never seen a girl defend herself? I'm southern, bitch. On your feet!"

She offered her hand and jerked him up. He fumbled with the gun as the two of them crashed down the hill, deeper into the shadows. The sky grew darker by the moment as the snowfall increased from a steady shower into a howling swirl. Banks panted as she ran beside him, and they stumbled over fallen logs and small depressions in the ground.

Reed's stomach twisted in panic. He could make out the shadowy figure of the shooter behind them a hundred yards back. He saw the rising muzzle of a rifle and the tilt of the killer's head as he leaned into the stock of his weapon.

A fresh string of gunfire tore through the forest. The ground gave way, and Reed tumbled backward, free-falling down a new hillside, rolling head over heels as Banks tumbled down beside him, scraping past trees and sliding through valleys of leaves. Snow and mud clogged his vision as he tumbled down the hill, rocks and fallen logs slamming into his shoulders as he slid and rolled toward the valley floor.

The gunshots faded. He swung his arm to the left, and a rock tore at his hand as he tried to locate Banks, but she was gone. A splash and then a shriek from Banks came moments before the frigid water closed around his own shoulders—and then his face.

Kicking and fighting to the surface, the chill from the wind was a distant memory as the immediate, cutting cold of the water sank straight to his bones. Frigid air whistled between his teeth as his head broke the surface. He kicked out with both legs, treading water for a moment before his head descended beneath the surface again.

They had fallen into a creek. He couldn't tell how wide or how deep as he fought to keep himself above the surface, but the saturating cold told him all he needed to know about their situation. They had only minutes to live if they remained in the water.

No. I won't die here.

His head broke the surface again, and he struck out with both legs, kicking toward the bank. "Banks!" He pulled himself out of the water and back onto the mud, coughing up water and bits of ice.

It was almost dark now, and he couldn't see more than five feet ahead. The snow was a thick blanket, almost as impenetrable as fog. His whole torso was racked with violent shivers as his body fought back hypothermia. But there were no more gunshots.

"Banks! Where are you?"

Reed dug for the flashlight in his pocket. He knew the bright LED was little better than a flashing beacon, marking the killer's target stranded in the bottom of the creekbed, but he didn't care. He had to find Banks.

Charging through the creek, he swept the light along the far side of the bank. Trees and bushes, cloaked in snow next to the water, were now ghosts in the darkness. Amid chunks of ice, a limb drifted down the creek and over a short waterfall.

Then he saw her. Banks clung to a bush on the far side of the creek, not far from the waterfall. Gasping for air and kicking out with both feet, she fought the current as Reed launched himself through the water, fighting for footing as the powerful push of the water dragged him toward the drop-off.

"Hold on! I'm coming!" He clicked the light off and jumped for the creekside, ten yards upstream from Banks. Praying that the killer had lost them in the roar of the gathering blizzard, he grabbed a low-hanging tree limb and hauled himself out of the water. The snow that blasted Reed obscured his vision beyond more than a few feet. The killer couldn't hope to track them in this soup.

He clawed his way back onto solid ground, then ran toward Banks, who continued kicking against the water without screaming. She was smarter than that, he realized. The sopping wet blonde focused all of her energy on survival instead of wasting precious breaths on expressing her fear. But he could tell she was only moments from giving out.

Reed scooped Banks into his arms and hauled her forward onto dry ground as she coughed. Particles of ice had formed on her nose and eyebrows, and patches of her face were flushed blue.

"Hold on, Banks. I've got you."

She staggered to her feet and spat creek water out between blue lips. "C-c-cold," she whispered.

Reed struggled with the zipper of her jacket, then ripped it with a powerful jerk. She fought him, huddling closer into the sopping garment.

"Take it off, Banks! Hypothermia will get you long before you freeze."

A fresh blast of wind tore straight through his body as he ripped off his own jacket. His torso felt frozen, and he pulled her close, rubbing her arms and back, and trying to keep the shirt from freezing to her skin. Nothing compared to the desperation he felt. Not the roar of gunfire snapping at his heels as he hurled himself off a cliff. Not the panic of the truck failing to start as The Wolf stared him down. Her life was here, in the balance.

Reed smacked her gently on the cheeks. "Banks! Stay with me. Focus!"

"I can't . . . breathe."

"Find a way, dammit. You wimpy Mississippi—"

Banks shoved him back, spraying creek water over the ground. The whites of her eyes were laced with red around pools of perfect blue. "When you almost drown, you can't breathe!" she snapped. "That's how that works!"

A hint of red returned to her cheeks—not enough to drive back encroaching hypothermia, but enough to bring hope into his desperate heart. Reed's mind raced, but he felt locked by indecision.

What now?

"What are you looking at?" Banks's words fell over one another as though she were drunk, but she gestured toward the forest. "Do something!"

Do something. Find shelter.

Reed wiped his face and peered down the creek into the whistle of wind and winter. Far ahead, nestled amongst the storm-torn brush, he caught sight of something mechanical.

"This way!" He took her arm and pulled her close, dragging her wet jacket along with him as they started through the trees. "Keep moving."

They crashed down the bank while Reed held the flashlight at eye level, spitting snow and feeling the tension grow in his body. He negotiated the side of the hill beside the waterfall. He had to find shelter immediately—a cave, or a recess between the hills—someplace he could build a fire and fight back against hypothermia. Banks wouldn't last much longer as the temperature dropped and the snow gathered around her ankles. Hell, *he* wouldn't last much longer. They needed shelter first, and then warmth. Without both, it would be less than half an hour before the forest swallowed them into the belly of the blizzard.

Reed's foot struck something hard, and it rang with

a *thunk*. Momentary elation was drowned by disappointment as he shone the light down onto the object. It was an overturned canoe, left in the mud between the trees and bushes, and not wide enough to provide even a hint of shelter from the cold that sank into his bones and tore the life from his blood.

We're going to die. She's going to die, right here in my arms.

The cherry-red was gone from her face, leaving behind a blue that was rapidly turning to pure white.

No, dammit. Not here.

"Banks, run. You have to run now!"

Her eyes gleamed up at his. With a voice barely strong enough to carry over the wind, she said, "Where?"

Reed pulled her closer to his side and shined light through the trees. Each second that ticked by felt like a drip of life flowing from his bones. Only moments remained. He searched between the trees for any hint of a path.

Nobody leaves a canoe in the middle of nowhere.

There had to be some kind of camp or maybe a cabin nearby. As he peered into the snow, the outline of a narrow clearing between the trees appeared, leading away from the canoe and deeper into the storm.

"This way," he said.

16

The onslaught of the blizzard was overwhelming. Clouds of snow obscured the path, encircling them like the bodies of a million ghosts. Even with the bright LED, the path between the trees became harder to see with every step. Desperation overwhelmed Reed's mind as he pressed forward, kicking through the bushes and crashing over small depressions. For all he knew, they were running in circles. At any moment, they might collide with a tree or run off the edge of a cliff, but he couldn't stop moving. A moment lost in the single-digit temperatures could mean death for them both.

"Hold on, Banks. Stay with me."

Banks shivered like a puppy stepping out of a cold bath. Her hands were frozen in place around his arm, and her face was twisted into a pucker of pain and fear. "Hell of a third d-d-date."

Reed pulled her closer and turned a corner around a tree, tripping over something and feeling pain rip through his shin. He shined the light on his feet, where a chunk of wood lay on the ground. It wasn't a tree limb or a rotting log—it was a piece of firewood.

The glow of the flashlight illuminated the swirling snow as Reed scanned the small clearing. He saw a splitting stump near the fallen firewood, and a little farther, a rusty steel barbecue grill like the ones in a state park, planted in the hard clay, leaning to one side. Across the far side of the clearing, nestled against the trees and almost obscured by the blizzard, a cabin squatted under the storm as though even it were freezing beneath the blast of the wind. Snow piled against its walls, and debris battered its single wooden door framed between boarded-up windows. It was built of pine logs with a cedar shingle roof—nothing as fancy as Oliver's A-frame, but to Reed it was the best-looking cabin he'd ever seen.

"Walk with me, Banks!"

His heart pounded, and Reed wondered if the cabin was locked. Was there somebody inside? Was the gunman still on their tail? None of that really mattered if he couldn't get them both out of the storm.

The latch was locked. Reed slammed against the pinewood door, framed by thick pine boards and hanging on heavy iron hinges, and was met by stiff resistance. He slammed his hand against the latch, but still, it didn't budge.

"Stand here, Banks." Reed placed her against the wall, then crashed into the door. Once. Twice. The blast of the wind tore so hard at his torso it almost pushed him off balance. Panic and sudden rage overtook his mind. It wasn't going to end this way. He'd rather fall on one of those damn grenades than watch Banks die.

Wood met flesh with a sickening thud as Reed slammed all two hundred thirty pounds of his body into the door. It crashed open with a splintering sound, and Reed fell inside onto the hardwood floor. His head smacked the planks, and the flashlight rolled out of his hand. He gasped for air, then rolled over and crawled back to his feet.

Banks huddled against the wall, but there was a smile dancing at the corners of her lips. "Not bad, Cowboy."

Reed hoisted her up and dragged her inside, then slammed the door shut. An entire chunk of it was missing around where the latch had been, and there was nothing to hold it closed. It blew open again, and Reed cursed. Why couldn't *anything* be easy?

He retrieved the flashlight and scanned the cabin's single room. Dust clung to the stained surface of each post on a worn, four-poster bed. Black ashes covered two rocking chairs next to a fireplace. The floor creaked under each footstep, and as he shined the flashlight toward the left half of the cabin, the pool of light illuminated a short counter and two cabinets with doors hanging on crooked hinges. The only other articles in the room were a table leaning on uneven legs and a large chest with drawers hanging half-open. Clothes spilled out, all dusty and old like nobody had entered this place for years.

Reed leaned against the dresser, sure it was loaded

with bricks. He strained, and as it slid a couple inches, his back screamed in pain.

Banks stumbled beside him and placed her shaking hands against the chest. "On three," she whispered. "One Mississippi, two Miss—"

Reed broke into a soft laugh. "Just push, Banks!"

They slid the chest until it slammed into the broken door. The sound of the wind beating against the side of the cabin was muted now, even though the window panes still rattled in their frames. The cabin was dark except for the glow of the flashlight, and now that the door was finally sealed, it felt strangely still inside.

Reed panted and collapsed on top of the chest, his arms still trembling from the bitter cold. Banks slumped against the wall, and for a moment, they relished the peace. The relief from the wind was palpable. Reed said a silent prayer of thanks for the miracle of the cabin. He wasn't sure if anyone was listening way up there above the blizzard. He wasn't sure if he cared. He just wanted to breathe.

The stone fireplace held a rusting metal grate inside a hearth about a foot deep. Next to a large stack of firewood was a can labeled *"flammable."* He knelt on the hard floor and piled firewood onto the grate as a bug scuttled out of the stack. Reed tilted the can over the wood, and a clear liquid streamed out, splashing on the timbers and turning them a dark brown. From the first sniff, Reed recognized the acidic odor of kerosene.

Banks rubbed her hands together over the hearth, as though crimson flames were already bursting from the fireplace.

"Lean back," Reed warned as he peeled off a strip of bark and splashed kerosene over one end. He pried the lighter out of his pocket and flicked it with his stiff thumb, but the flint ground with a squishy sound. The lighter was still sopping wet from the creek.

Reed ground his thumb into the flint again. Once. Twice. Sparks flew from the wheel, then a flame burst from the mouth of the lighter. Reed waved it under the tip of the bark, gratified to see flames rising from the wood and sending a pale flash of heat over his face.

The bark found its home in the fireplace, and golden fire erupted from the grate, engulfing the logs and sending warmth rushing from the hearth. Banks and Reed huddled so close together that the flames almost licked their faces. Every tiny wave of heat was like heaven washing over their bodies and pouring life into their frozen veins. Banks's ice-encrusted hair dangled over the hearth.

"Damn that feels good." Banks rubbed her hands together in front of the flames. A hint of red returned to her cheeks, ushered on by a growing smile. That smile ignited a warmth someplace deep inside of him that was stronger than any fire ever could be. He didn't understand it. He had never felt it before. Even with Kelly and their whirlwind romance, it didn't feel this way—this felt stable and deep.

Reed watched as she combed the melting snow out of her hair. Each twist of her fingers around blonde waves produced new flakes raining down over the floorboards, there to melt under the rising temperature. She fought with a stick tangled in her bangs, and for a moment, the smile faded.

Reed touched her hand, and she froze as her bright eyes met his. The flames in the hearth reflected in her crystal gaze, unbroken by the scourge of the blizzard.

"Let me," he whispered.

Her hands fell away from the knot of hair, and Reed twisted his fingers against the stick. It broke, then hit the floor as her liberated bangs fell over a damp forehead. He lowered his hand, still admiring her glistening face. She touched her fingers to his, and the lightning bolt that ripped through his body poured gasoline onto the warmth he already felt, turning a glowing ember into a raging fire. It numbed the pain and muted the wind, leaving only the beautiful woman kneeling on the floor beside him. It was a moment too perfect, too warm for any storm to break.

Whoever is up there . . . thank you.

17

Western North Carolina

T he Glock hung faithfully at Reed's side, water dripping from the barrel. He unsnapped the retainer and dropped the magazine. Eight rounds left. The spare magazines were in the jacket pocket, somewhere outside, buried in the snow.

Shit.

Reed blew the water from the muzzle, then jammed the magazine back into the gun. There was no need to worry about the moisture—the durable weapon would dry quickly by the fire. Reed dropped the shoulder holster on the table, then pulled his T-shirt, dripping with creek water, up and over his head. Banks's mouth dropped open.

He coughed and looked away. "Sorry. It needs to dry."

"Oh my God." She hurried across the living room and placed her hand against his chest, tracing the dark bruises from around his side to the tear in his flesh. "Is this from the train?"

He'd mostly forgotten about the bruises. Some were from the train. Others were from the gunfight at the FBI field office the week prior. And, of course, the new ones were from the fall off the cliff the night before. They covered his torso like spots on a cow, both irregular and pervasive.

"Yeah. It's fine."

Reed pulled away but felt a sudden touch on his ribcage. Banks stepped closer. She laid eyes on him without reservation, but he could see questions, the sharp wit of a woman who wasn't fooled.

"You're not a venture capitalist, are you?"

Reed rubbed the back of his neck. "I invest in a lot of things."

"Things that get you shot up in a dollar store parking lot?"

Her stare exposed the simple soul deep within her. Not stupid. Not shallow. Just simple. The kind of simplicity that saw the world as it was and took life one day at a time—a happy, realistic simple. A simple he didn't understand.

"That was just a misunderstanding. That guy, um .. . he's grouchy."

She folded her arms. "Well, I hope he has insurance. Somebody owes me a Beetle."

"I'm sorry about that. I'll replace it."

"Are you sure you can afford it?" She ran her fingertips up his arm, stroking the outlines of a half-dozen scars. Her eyes danced with distant fire and not a hint of fear.

"I don't have the cash *on me*," he said.

"Is that right? Have to arrange a payment plan, won't you?"

"I guess . . ." Reed's words trailed off as he lost himself in her gaze. Wit and intelligence still shone in those bright eyes, but nothing else clouded her gaze. It was deep and honest and totally open. As though she wanted him to see her not just for what she was, but who she was. What she felt.

Banks ran her hand behind his neck and pressed her lips against his. Every bit as strong and over-whelming as he remembered, the kiss sent waves of thrill, fear, and elation rushing through his body like no drug ever could. She pulled his body into hers. Her hands were strong and soft and warm, running up his back and behind his neck.

He sank closer into her embrace as the moments stretched out, distorting his perception of passing time. Their clothes fell to the floor, and he slid his hands over each perfect curve of her naked body glowing in the firelight. Renewed passion surged into his mind, and the room around him faded from view as he pulled her closer, kissing her as long and slow as he had that first night in Atlanta. As she kissed him back, he heard the breath rush into her lungs and felt her body come alive. Her arm slid behind his back, and they tumbled to the floor next to the fireplace. He was vaguely aware of the dirt and grime that covered the floorboards, but he didn't care.

He lay on the hard floor as she moved on top of him with gentle twists of her curved form, cries of passion escaping her lips. Reed closed his eyes as her fingers slid between his. Every brush of her skin unleashed new levels of pleasure. The ache in his bones was driven back, overwhelmed by warmth and love. He slid his hand behind her neck and sat up, pulling her in for another kiss before rolling over on top of her. Banks closed her eyes and bit her lip. Firelight danced across the floorboards and sparkled against the melting snow on her cheeks. He lost himself in her face, memorizing every curve, every line and perfect detail. His mind faded back to the moment at the top of that parking garage in Atlanta, the moment when her beauty and grace enchanted him. Every deep longing that was awakened at that moment, then imprisoned as he walked away from the hospital, burst free from deep in his heart and overwhelmed his soul. He needed this woman. He adored this woman. She was the first thing in his entire life that felt completely safe. Completely home.

The rush of passion grew so strong his mind went numb, but beneath it all, he felt something else—something stronger and more stable. Something he hadn't felt in twenty years: belonging. It felt right in this moment—deep and real. Being with Banks, being close to her, sharing every intimacy, he was risking his entire shadowy persona to a person he really didn't even know, yet he felt like he'd known her his whole life. No matter the bloodshed or the money or the endless mountaintops of accomplishment he put beneath his feet, he couldn't outrun the reality that something was missing—something like Banks.

He kissed her neck and shoulders and pulled her body closer to his, drinking in each moment—the electric pleasure tearing through his body more powerful than a bullet.

He pressed his lips against her cheek and held her close. Held her like he'd never let go.

———

Banks rested her head on his bare chest. "Is your name really Chris?"

Reed lay back on the bed, enjoying the warmth and relaxation of the fire. Her voice, as soft and pure as her skin, sounded like music—like a waterfall trickling into a quiet valley.

"No." Why did he say that? He couldn't tell her his real name—it wasn't safe for either of them. But something in his soul wouldn't allow him to lie.

"I didn't think so." She stroked his stomach. "Are you going to tell me your name?"

This time he waited before answering, savoring the touch of her fingers on his skin. "I liked Cowboy. You could call me that."

She laughed. "I don't think I can call you *boy* after a performance like that."

He smiled but left his eyes closed, running his hand over her exposed back. She moved in closer, and for a moment, the only sounds that joined the crackling of the fire were their gentle breaths.

"Where are you from?" she asked.

"I was born in Birmingham."

"England?"

Reed snorted, and she giggled. "Alabama. But I grew up in Los Angeles. Moved there when I was ten."

"Your parents still live there?"

"My mother does. I haven't been back in a while."

"And your father?"

Once more, Reed hesitated, then relaxed. "He's elsewhere."

"I see." Maybe she knew when to stop pressing, or maybe she was saving it for later. "So, how did you wind up in Atlanta?"

"I was a Marine. Served overseas for a while. . . . Iraq, mostly."

"Is that where you got the scars?"

"Some of them."

He stroked her hair, pushing it behind her ears and over her shoulders. She lay perfectly still with her cheek on his chest. He couldn't see her face, but he imagined that her eyes were closed.

"After I left the military . . . well, lots of things happened. I went into business for myself, found my way to Atlanta, and . . . I guess it just seemed like a place to land. So here I am."

"Here you are . . . investing in billion-dollar firms in the middle of the Appalachian wilderness." She ran her finger down the center of his chest.

He could hear the sarcasm in her voice, but it wasn't cutting. It was honest, like everything else about her. She knew he was lying, and she wanted him to know she knew, but she wasn't going to press it. Not now. Reed was grateful for that. He didn't want to lie to her. Something about her open sincerity made him want to tell her everything, to spill his guts and shed every mask he'd ever worn.

But he couldn't. He never could. Not only would he lose her, he'd lose himself.

Reed shifted against the bed and cleared his throat. "Okay, your turn. What's your story?"

She sighed. "My story? I'm afraid it's pretty dull, honestly."

"I doubt it."

"Why do you say that?"

Reed shrugged. "I've met a lot of people in my line of work. None of them have dull stories."

She lay still, and her chest rose and fell in gentle waves. "I was born in Tupelo."

"Hence the sexy accent."

She laughed. "Yeah . . . hence a lot of things."

"So, who were your parents?"

"My parents were wealthy. My mother is heir to this big oil business out in Texas. Extended family are all multimillionaires, but I don't know much about them. I just know she always had a lot of money. She liked to spend it, too. We lived in this giant house on a small estate, and they called it a plantation, which is pretty standard in Mississippi, I guess, but it always bothered me. I always felt like a rich white girl living it up in the rural south, surrounded by some of the poorest people in the country. I mean, my first car was a Maserati. At fifteen."

"No shit?" Nothing about the woman lying in his arms impressed him as being a spoiled rich girl.

"Yeah, I never liked it. All my friends had pickup trucks and old beat-up Mustangs. We used to go down to the river and drink, skinny-dip under the moonlight, and smoke cigarettes. Mom would've killed me had she known. She wanted me to graduate and go to an Ivy League school and study law or something. Prep me to be the next heir to the family empire."

"I'm guessing you had other plans."

"No, I was going to do it. I had applications at half a dozen schools in the northeast. I was already looking for apartments."

"What happened?"

"My father . . ." Her voice broke. "My father died. He was on business in New Orleans and was hit by a drunk driver. They say he died instantly. . . . I hope it's true. He was such a good man—a kind, gentle soul. He spoiled me rotten, but not like my mother did with money and things. Daddy really spent time with me. We would sneak out and get ice cream and watch movies when I was a kid, and when I was in high school, he would take me to Memphis, and we'd slip into bars and drink. He was cool like that. He said I was his girl. That was all he ever called me, actually—'*my girl.*'"

Banks sucked in a deep breath, and her fingers tightened around his skin.

Reed spoke softly. "What did he do?"

"He was a doctor, but not like a physician. I mean, he had a medical degree, but it was mostly research. He was always driving up to Nashville and working at

Vanderbilt. I like to think he did a lot of good in the world."

He squeezed her shoulder. "I know he did. What was his name?"

"Francis."

Reed's brow wrinkled. The name sounded vaguely familiar, as though he had heard it recently, but he couldn't place it.

"After he was buried, Mom became horrible, working all the time and always flying to Texas. She was really mean and intense about me going to school. I guess I just broke down. I ran out late one night and took a bus to Atlanta to see my godfather—Senator Holiday—the one you met in the hospital. He and Daddy were close friends. I stayed with him a while, and then I just knew I wanted to be on my own. I was sick of being the rich girl everybody takes care of. I wanted to take care of myself, chase my music, and just be alive for a while. And that's about it. That's my story, I guess. See? I told you it was boring." Her laugh was soft.

He nestled his head close to hers, then kissed her forehead. "Not for a moment."

18

Reed slipped out of bed, leaving Banks sleeping in a curled-up ball. His dry clothes smelled of river water and smoke, and they stuck to his skin as he pulled them on.

I wish I could stay in bed with her forever.

The fire had gone out in the night, and now the cabin lay in stillness as cold air seeped through the crack beneath the door. Reed peered out of the window. A field of white blanketed the woods around them, broken only by the tall grey trunks of the trees that shot toward the sky. Snow was built up at least a foot outside the cabin, laying in thick drifts where the wind had left it.

Reed's stomach growled, and the bed creaked behind him. Banks sat up, and her blonde hair fell in tangled waves. She smiled, and without a word began to dress in front of the vacant fireplace.

Reed rifled through the cabinets, searching for

anything edible, though all he could find were a couple old cans of baked beans. He cut the lids open with the tip of his knife, then handed one can to Banks, who sat at the table and ate the beans without comment, scooping them out of the can with her fingers.

"No utensils?" she asked.

Reed sat down across from her and dug his fingers into the sticky beans. "Just the one I used last night. I still have it on me if you're interested."

She rolled her eyes. "Too big for the can."

Reed grinned and shoveled more beans into his mouth. They were ancient but didn't taste half bad. Through a mouthful, he said, "You never told me why you're here."

Banks grunted. "My godfather has a cabin a few miles from where you found me. After that stuff in Atlanta, the FBI thought it would be a good idea for him to get out of town for a while, so I drove up for a visit."

Godfather. Holiday.

Reed wanted to kick himself. He remembered reading in Holiday's file that he owned a vacation cabin up here in the mountains, but even as Reed journeyed to hunt Oliver, he never considered the possibility that Holiday may have retreated to the cabin.

Not that it should have mattered either way, really. Not until Reed ran into Banks.

He finished the beans and set the can on the table. For a moment, he stared at the girl sitting cross-legged next to him, and his mind was lost in her simple beauty.

But not just her beauty—her mental fortitude, also. He marveled that this woman, who had endured a brutal kidnapping only two weeks prior, and now was huddled inside a cabin in the middle of nowhere after running for her life from a maddened killer with a grenade launcher, could be so composed and calm. He wondered how that could be natural. Were he in her shoes, with no prior experience in warfare or bloodshed, he would be freaking out right now. Did she not grasp the reality of the terror that had befallen her, or was she simply that much stronger than he realized?

Banks looked up and lifted one eyebrow. "What?"

He shook his head and rubbed his fingers against the table, smearing the bean residue off his skin. He pushed away the confused thoughts about Banks and forced himself to refocus on the problem at hand. Or, rather, the *problems*. There were several of them.

After escaping The Wolf in the woods, his focus had been staying alive long enough to find Oliver. Now that goal seemed even further out of reach. If Mitch Holiday were in these mountains, it was only a matter of time before Oliver knew about it, and after that, the senator would be anything but safe. Whoever The Wolf worked for, he might be just as interested in killing Holiday as he was in burying Reed.

"I think you should leave me here." Banks leaned back in her chair, her arms folded as she stared out the window.

"What?"

"Whoever ran us off the road will be back. You

should probably get back to town before he finds us. He won't hurt me."

The calm frankness of her words took him off guard, and he wondered for a minute if she was completely ignorant of the severity of their situation. But no, she wasn't dumb. She was just rational.

"I think we should get you back to your godfather, first."

Banks shrugged. "I can see to that. Where are we, anyway?"

Reed twisted his neck until it popped, then scooped up the cans and walked them to the empty trash bin in the corner. "I'm not sure. Either North Carolina or Tennessee. We were pretty close to the state line when we wrecked. Robbinsville is east of here."

"Are there any highways?"

"Highways? No. State roads, maybe. Places where we could pick up a ride."

"What about the Beetle?" she said.

Reed lifted Banks's bright red coat off the counter and dusted it off. It was mostly dry from the night before. "The Beetle is beyond the help of AAA, I'm afraid. We'll have to walk."

Banks slid the jacket on, then wrapped it around her slim body before standing on her tiptoes and kissing him on the lips.

"Well, all right, then. Let's roll, Cowboy."

The forest outside the cabin was a winter wonderland, a field of frozen trunks buried in drifts of perfect white. Reed had no clue where the nearest road lay or how to get back to a main highway. For all he knew, they would have to walk miles before encountering any life. He guessed that the cabin wouldn't be too far from civilization, so they started through the trees. Birds flitted, tweeting to one another as they swooped down between limbs and played in the snow. An occasional chipmunk bounded in the soft white snow, staring with beady eyes at the human invaders as they trudged onward. There was something perfectly serene about this place, now muted with snow and accented with icy diamonds.

Miles passed before the trees parted at a hilltop, and Reed caught sight of a two-lane roadbed a hundred yards below. It was covered in a thin sheet of snow, but tire marks ran back and forth in both lanes. There was traffic, at least, and maybe it wouldn't be long before the next vehicle happened along.

The exact position of the sun was difficult to determine through the mountaintops and trees, but hoping they were headed east, they faced the general direction of the light and marched on.

Banks looped her arm through his, her cheeks now flushed. "So. Coke or Pepsi?"

Reed laughed. "What?"

"It's a game I read about one time. Twenty questions to learn about a person—or, you know . . . a lover."

Reed shot her a sideways look. "Is that what I am now?"

"Well, you're definitely not a venture capitalist, so . . ."

He looked away. "Okay, fine. Coke."

"Ooh, nice."

"You?"

"Mountain Dew."

He poked her in the arm. "That wasn't an option."

She shrugged. "What can I say? I'm a rule breaker."

"Clearly. Ask me another."

She pursed her lips and looked up at the tree limbs hanging over the road. "Beach or mountains?"

"Beach. All day. You?"

"Same. Florida coast. Destin is my spot. Sports or movies?"

"Sports. Baseball and drag racing."

She giggled. "Yeah, don't quit your day job. You suck at racing."

"Well, if I had a decent car." He jabbed at her, but she moved to the side and danced backward, her hands in her pockets as she stared at him.

"Okay," she said. "Now for the tough ones. Don't think, just answer. Red or blue?"

"Red."

"Cold or hot?"

"Hot."

"Men or women?"

"Wait . . . what?" He wrinkled his brow, and she laughed, her eyes alight as she skipped backward, her feet moving over the road with deft accuracy. Her laugh was so light and gentle. Reed had never heard a sound so lovely. So much like home.

He broke into a run, pounding through the pavement as she slid to the side. His arms closed around her stomach, and he hoisted her off the ground, cradling her in his arms in the middle of the roadway. Bits of fresh snowfall stuck to her hair as she stared at him, her smile wide and bright. Reed kissed her, and she kissed back, wrapping her hand around his neck and pressing in close.

Tires ground on the pavement behind them. Reed flinched and jammed his hand beneath the jacket, wrapping his fingers around the grip of the Glock. His feet were rooted to the ground as the rumble of a big motor pounded closer. A lifted pickup truck hummed down the road behind them, its diesel engine rumbling over the asphalt. Reed relaxed his shoulders and held out his hand, thumb up. The truck bounced to a stop, and the passenger side window slid down. Even from his six-foot-four vantage point, Reed could barely see inside the cab.

"You folks lost?" The big man in the cab wore camouflage hunting clothes and a bright orange hat. His wide smile was missing teeth, but it was friendly.

"We broke down a few miles back, and we're trying to get back to town. Mind giving us a lift?"

"Which town?"

Reed shrugged and offered his most disarming smile. "Dunno. We're traveling through. Not exactly sure where we are."

Banks shoved Reed out of the way and hopped up

onto the truck's running board before he could stop her. She shoved her head into the cab and offered her hand to the driver. "Hell of a rig you got here. You ever run biodiesel in this baby?"

The big man grinned. "What, you a motorhead? Climb in, darlin'. I'll get y'all back to the big city."

19

Lake Santeetlah, North Carolina

As it turned out, the "big city" was Fontana Dam, a tiny community nestled in northern Graham County, with a resident population of thirty people. George, their driver, was planning to do some shopping at the local general store. But by the time they rolled into the little community, Banks had him so warmed up talking about engines that he readily agreed to drive them another thirty minutes in the opposite direction, to Lake Santeetlah, a booming metropolis, population forty-three.

Reed rode in the back seat, jammed up next to a pile of smelly hunting clothes, while Banks took shotgun, carrying on a boisterous conversation with George about the understated performance power of diesels and their unappreciated racing capacity.

Banks's thorough understanding of engines was impressive. At the time, Reed assumed Banks's opening comment to George was designed simply to disarm him and secure their ride, but he quickly realized she had a genuine interest in the subject. Her technical knowledge of motors and performance, while a lot different than Reed's, was nonetheless enchanting.

How many times in a lifetime do you meet somebody like this? Somebody so sincere, and happy, and content with themselves?

As they piled out of the truck, George called after Banks, adding some last-minute wisdom about turbo-diesels. Banks waved, and George turned his toothy grin toward Reed, addressing him for the first time since picking them up.

"You take care of her. You hear me, boy? Got a good un, right there!"

The truck roared and bounced off. Standing at the edge of the small town, Reed shot Banks an inquisitive look.

She laughed and shrugged. "What? I told you I'm a southern girl."

The town of Lake Santeetlah sat right next to the water and consisted of a small gathering of homes and shops. Banks explained that Holiday's cabin sat fifty yards off the water, halfway back to Robbinsville.

Once again, the sky boiled with muddy grey clouds, sweeping in from the west over the mountains. Another snowfall was coming—maybe a bigger one. Reed didn't like the idea of staying with Banks while The Wolf was still on the prowl, but it was probably the best option if the weather took a turn for the worse. Because of the cold, there were no boats out on the lake, but Banks found a local with a pontoon boat down by the dock, and Reed paid him forty bucks to ferry them to Holiday's place.

As the water lapped and churned against the bottom of the boat, Reed stood at the bow with his arms crossed and tried to force his mind to relax. He didn't like crossing the open water, fully exposed this way, but he liked the idea of walking the narrow mountain roads even less. With luck, The Wolf was still snowed in ten miles to the west, and that would buy him enough time to get Banks to safety.

"Let her go, Reed . . . I saw the look in your eyes when you said her name. Take it from me . . . you break hearts a lot better than you break necks."

Kelly's warning echoed in his mind as he glanced back at Banks sitting next to the driver, chatting it up about fishing in the winter. The pilot was as engaged with her as George had been, laughing and motioning with his hands as he disclosed all of his secret fishing spots.

She's unlike anyone else on the planet—even Kelly.

Kelly. She was a lot of things—wild, ferocious, somewhat abrasive—but she had rarely been wrong in the two years he'd known her. Their love, for however long it lasted, felt real. Maybe it even felt like the kind of thing lifelong partnerships were made of, but looking back now, Reed could see the gaping cracks in their union. It was never meant to last, yet he put a lot of faith in Kelly's opinion. Her condemnation of his interest in Banks shook the foundation of the longing that boiled in his soul. Ever since David Montgomery was hauled off to prison and Tabitha dragged her son to the far side of the country, Reed never felt at home. But here, standing on this boat and watching Banks laugh . . . it felt more like home than anything he remembered.

Reed rested on the railing and watched the black water ripple and churn under the pontoons, vanishing from sight beneath the deck of the boat. Life was like that: It was here, so vibrant and active and beautiful, and then it was gone, swept away, and vanishing into the darkness of the world around it.

Banks can't be swept away like that.

He made the choice at the hospital to walk out and leave Banks standing in the hallway with tears streaming down her beautiful face. He remembered *why* he made that choice, and the reality of his situation hadn't changed.

I'll get her to Holiday. Make sure they're both safe again. Deal with The Wolf and deal with Oliver. And then I'll disappear. She deserves that.

The boat's motor whined down as the pilot allowed the pontoon to glide the last twenty yards until it ground against the muddy bank of the lake. Banks gave the driver a fist-bump, then walked through the front gate and jumped ashore. Reed waved at the pilot and followed, looking to the cabin that sat at the top of a hill.

It was nothing short of spectacular—obviously kit-built, but still refined. Giant red logs formed an A-frame sheathed in dark green sheet metal. Glass lined the front of the cabin, facing out toward the water and exposing a brightly lit interior on the other side. A tall man wearing a dark grey uniform and carrying an assault rifle stood by the door, monitoring the lake as though it were the most boring view in the universe.

Banks slid her fingers between his, and he looked down at her soft white hand.

God, this woman.

She pulled him up the hill, and Reed followed without protest, nodding at the guard once before Banks opened the door.

"Uncle! I'm back!"

A clattering sound rang from the other end of the cabin, and Mitch Holiday appeared at the door. He wore loose blue jeans and a turtleneck shirt, and his hair was perfectly combed back—the picture of political composure. But beneath that practiced pose of collection, the clear traces of Holiday's recent misfortunes were evident—bruises still clouded one cheek, and his right knee bulged beneath the blue jeans where a hefty brace encased it. Reed remembered what had happened to that knee—remembered the sickening crack of bone caving in as Holiday fell off the ladder outside the FBI field office.

It was a wonder Holiday could walk at all. The man must be tougher than he looked.

"Banks!" Holiday limped across the living room and wrapped her in a tight hug.

Reed scanned the small cabin, noting the pile of legal documents heaped on the coffee table next to an open laptop. A gas fire burned in the hearth, sending silent flames dancing amongst fireproof logs. His stomach growled, and he turned back to the senator.

Holiday still held Banks close to his chest, both arms wrapped around her shoulders. "My God, girl. I was so worried. Where the hell did you go?"

Banks turned to Reed. "Oscar broke down, but look who I found!"

Holiday looked up, his eyes settling on Reed for the first time. His gaze was clouded by uncertainty for a moment, quickly melting into a warm smile. "Chris!" He wrapped his long and powerful arms around Reed in a big bear hug.

Reed stood awkwardly while the senator finished the hug, then watched Holiday stumble back. He moved slowly, with pain flashing in his eyes. Thick bandages were visible, wadded up beneath the turtleneck and over the wounds he still didn't know Reed had inflicted.

"How are you, Senator?"

Holiday sighed. "I'm better, Chris. Got this shit patched up and getting back to work now. You can see they've got me bottled up here like a prisoner. But that's part of it, I suppose."

Banks gave Holiday's arm a squeeze, then hurried past him toward the open kitchen. "We haven't eaten. What's for lunch?"

Holiday waved her aside. "Get out of here. I'm fixing lunch. Chris! You like steak?"

"Sure." Reed sat down at the bar and bit back a grunt. Flashes of new pain pulsated through his torso, erupting from the bruises and cuts that crisscrossed his ribcage. Taking another one of Kelly's pills would only cause exhaustion, and he couldn't afford that. He needed to focus now.

Holiday limped about the kitchen, throwing pots on the stove and digging in the fridge. Banks sat beside Reed and put her head on his shoulder. Once again, he marveled at her composure and calmness. She had just been shot at, run through the woods, almost drowned, and starved to death. Yet here she was, relaxed and warm, acting as though nothing in the world could steal her peace.

This woman was bulletproof.

"Why did you lie?" Reed whispered beneath the clang of pots.

"About what?"

"What happened in the woods?"

Banks shrugged. "Because I still don't know the truth."

Fair answer.

Reed adjusted himself on the stool, then cleared his throat. "Could I borrow a phone, Senator? Mine is dead."

"Mitch. Call me Mitch. And sure, mine's on the table."

Reed smiled at Banks, then scooped up the phone and stepped back through the door. The guard cast him a casual, uninterested glance, then resumed his surveillance of the lake. Reed walked into the woods, putting enough distance between himself and the guard to prevent his voice from traveling, and then he dialed.

"Winter."

"Don't hang up."

The line went silent, then Winter snapped back with a hint of venom. "I told you not to call me again. I can't get involved in your little war."

"This isn't about that. I have another question. Legitimate business. Will you talk to me?"

Winter's silence was noncommittal, but Reed took it as acceptance.

"I need a personnel file. Just a basic sum-up."

"Name?" Winter spat the word.

"I don't have a name. But I think he's called *The Wolf*."

Dead silence returned to the line, then grinding teeth resounded through the phone. "I *told you*, I'm not getting involved in this war of yours."

"So you know him? Who is he?"

"Somebody you really don't want to cross. Is that enough information for you?"

"Who does he work for? Oliver?"

Winter's groan was full of derision and impatience. This was more emotion than Reed had ever heard from Winter.

"Oliver couldn't afford him. He's a free agent. A top-shelf killer. Much better than Oliver's crew."

Reed leaned against a pine tree. "I'm flattered."

"And why is that?"

"Because he's trying to kill me."

"In that case, nice knowing you. This is the end of your rope."

"I'm not that easy to kill, Winter. What else can you tell me?"

"Only what I've already told you. You're in way over your head. Remember when I said so before? This is what I was talking about. Never call me again."

The line clicked off, and Reed stared down at the blank phone screen.

If he's not working for Oliver, who the hell is he working for?

Reed swiped at the number on the outbound call list, but there wasn't an option to delete it from the history. He cursed, then turned and smashed the phone against the tree. On the third strike the screen shattered.

Walking back toward the cabin, he kicked at the dirt, trying to make sense of Winter's evolving behavior. Was the ghost afraid, or was Winter simply maintaining absolute neutrality?

"I dropped your phone, Mitch." Reed set the busted device on the counter. "I'm sorry. I'll get you a new one."

Holiday looked down at the phone, a brief frown crossing his face. He flicked his hand in the air. "No worries, Chris. Grab a chair. Lunch's almost ready."

20

H oliday never stopped talking. He sawed through his steak, rattling on about everything from Georgia politics to peach ice cream, filling the meal with a steady stream of pontifications and musings. Every time he asked Reed or Banks a question, he took so long to clarify what he was asking that the actual inquiry was lost in the weeds. Reed took a sip of expensive craft beer, watching Holiday guzzle hundred-dollar bourbon while he launched into a dissertation on coastal shipping outside of Savannah. With each key point, he tapped the tip of his steak knife on the wooden table.

He's scared shitless. But why?

"And that's why I support local tariffs, you see? Everybody has to get paid."

Reed finished the beer and set the bottle on the table. "Do you spend a lot of time in Brunswick, Mitch?"

Holiday shook his head, pushing the plate back and

letting out a sigh. "Not as much as I'd like. Always in Atlanta these days."

"I thought the general assembly was almost finished for the year."

"Sure, we are. But then there's other work . . . Anyway, what do you do again?"

"I'm a day trader."

"I thought you said you invested in businesses?" Holiday's eyes were bloodshot, and his gaze seemed unfocused.

Reed shrugged. "Well, you know. . . . You don't put all your eggs in one basket, right?"

Holiday smacked the table. "Exactly! That's what I tell people all the time. You have to diversify. That's what I told them when . . ." He trailed off suddenly, then shook his head. "Wow, I think I've overindulged a little. My apologies, Chris. Would you like dessert? I was thinking maybe some peach—"

"Actually, Senator, I was hoping you had a cigar handy."

Holiday's eyes lit up like Christmas lights, and he broke into a grin. "A cigar man, eh? I knew I liked you. Let me fetch my humidor, and we'll step out on the porch."

Banks patted Reed on the hand. "I'm going to take a shower in something other than a creek. See you in a minute."

She kissed him on the cheek, her lips lingering a moment longer than was necessary. That warm rush flooded through his body again, and he closed his eyes.

Then she squeezed his arm and walked toward the bathroom.

Holiday reappeared from his bedroom, holding a small wooden box and a Zippo. Reed returned his smile, then stepped out onto the front porch. The guard had moved farther down the lot toward the lake and joined an identically dressed man carrying a shotgun. It was barely one in the afternoon, but the boiling clouds blocked the sun, leaving the surface of the water a churning black beneath the wind.

Reed accepted a cigar and snipped the end off with his teeth, then dangled the tip over Holiday's outstretched lighter. The smoke tasted sweet and strong, definitely Cuban, and well-aged. Reed took a long puff and wished like hell it was a cigarette instead.

"So tell me, Mitch. How long do they expect you to be up here?"

Holiday rolled the cigar between his fingers, then took a slow puff. "Who knows, kid. Nobody talks to me."

"Do they have any leads, at least?"

"Yeah . . ." Holiday stared at the lake with empty eyes. "Got some guy on videotape. The guy who busted me out of the FBI office. Working on running him down now."

"Well, I hope they find him."

Holiday just stared at the water over the front rail of the deck, wearing only the turtleneck but not shivering in the cutting cold.

"Why do you think they want you dead? Some legislative business?"

"No, nothing like that." Holiday stuffed the cigar back between his teeth and puffed, long and slow. Reed decided to wait for him to speak, trusting the alcohol in Holiday's blood more than his own ability to worm out the truth.

Holiday spoke in a low monotone, still staring into space. "You ever do something you think is the right thing and it just kind of . . . becomes something else?"

Reed grunted. "Yeah. Several times. What did you do?"

Holiday shook his head and closed his eyes. "Protected a friend. Somebody I would've died for. And then . . ." The words blended into the whistle of the wind on the water. Holiday took another puff on the cigar, then tilted his head toward Reed. "You sure we haven't met before? I swear there's something familiar about you."

Reed forced a smile and looked away. "You probably saw me at a fundraiser. I have some business down in Savannah."

"No shit. Well, proud to represent you."

"No offense, Senator. I voted for the other guy. But I'd vote for you next time."

Holiday laughed and jammed the cigar between his back teeth. "There won't be a next time, kid. If I ever get out of this cabin, I think it's time I retired and found a quieter life."

Reed watched him out of the corner of his eye, studying Holiday's every movement. The twitch of his eyes, the way he rubbed the railing with his right thumb. He radiated stress like a nuclear reactor.

"Well, I need a beer," Holiday said. "Can I get you anything?"

Reed knocked the ashes off the end of the cigar, then extinguished it against the railing. "Actually, I wondered if I could borrow your vehicle. I need to run to town and get some fresh clothes."

Holiday raised an eyebrow. "It's not going to end up in a ditch like my phone, is it?"

Reed laughed. "No worries, Senator. I'm a careful driver. I'll grab you some beer while I'm out."

Holiday's eyes lit up at that, and he waved the cigar toward Reed with a drunken flip of his hand. "You've got my vote, Chris Thomas! Here"—he dropped his keys into Reed's hand—"get a case."

Reed dumped the cigar into the snow, then jumped off the deck and hurried around the cabin to a jet-black Land Rover, mud and snow clinging to the fenders. It beeped once when he hit the unlocks, then roared to life as he slammed the door. He slid it into gear, then turned back down the drive and toward the highway.

It was time to find some answers.

21

Cherokee, North Carolina

F orty-five miles east of Lake Santeetlah lay
Cherokee, North Carolina. Predominantly a
tourist town, it was the closest city of significance that
could promise the refitting Reed required. It took him
over an hour to negotiate the narrow, slick mountain
roads, but once he reached the city limits, he replaced
his clothes at a department store, then purchased new
bandages, over-the-counter painkillers, and a
toothbrush.

A quick trip to a convenience store bathroom
allowed him to change clothes, wash the wound in his
side, and wrap it in gauze.

At an Internet café, he sat down at a computer with
a tall cup of coffee. In spite of the full night's rest, he
could feel the wear and tear of the last few days dragging at the edges of his consciousness, threatening to
pull him down. It was already growing dark outside as

the building bank of clouds suffocated the sunlight. Within the hour, full darkness would fall, making it even harder to keep awake and alert.

Holiday made a comment on the porch that finally connected two dots Reed had struggled with all afternoon. When Banks mentioned her father, Francis Morccelli, the name rang a bell, but he couldn't place the memory. Holiday's brief mention of a friend he tried to protect brought to mind Reed's last intense conversation with the senator, back in the trailer outside of Atlanta. Reed had kidnapped Holiday and interrogated him in that trailer while wearing a mask, but during the process, Holiday asked a peculiar question of his own. He said, *"Did you kill Frank?"*

Frank must've been Banks's father and Holiday's frat brother. Reed remembered Winter mentioning it two weeks prior when Reed first began to dig into Banks's identity. Winter had said Frank and Holiday attended Vanderbilt University together, birthing a friendship that lasted into their professional lives. Banks believed her father died at the hands of a drunk driver. But Holiday's morbid question while lying on the floor and staring into the eyes of his potential killer indicated otherwise.

Why does Holiday think Frank was murdered?

Reed searched online for *"Dr. Francis Morccelli."* The resulting listings were overwhelming—much as he anticipated. He narrowed the search by adding *"New Orleans"* to the field and found a local news article detailing the accident, dated June of 2013.

Dr. Francis D. Morccelli of Tupelo, MS, was tragically killed last night around 12:45 a.m. when an intoxicated driver lost control of his vehicle and hit Dr. Morccelli three blocks off of Bourbon Street. Dr. Morccelli is survived by his wife, Samantha, and his daughter, Banks.

Reed scanned the remainder of the article, but it recorded nothing helpful about the incident other than intended police investigations. He searched again for follow-up articles. *Why were you in New Orleans, Doctor?*

"He was always driving up to Nashville." Banks's words echoed in his mind, and he placed his fingers on the keys again. *"Dr. Morccelli, Vanderbilt, research, 2013."*

This time the results were much more specific. Research papers written by Frank were all available for public consumption on Vanderbilt's website. Apparently, Frank often partnered with Vanderbilt on research projects but wasn't directly employed by the university or the hospital. He specialized in pharmaceutical research and had a great many radical theories about the possibilities of DNA-inspired synthetic drugs.

". . . the epicenter of my theory is this—a genetic disease is, by its nature, caused and extrapolated by the mutant, damaged, or underdeveloped genes of the host subject. These genes are the factory wherein diseases of all sorts are birthed and fostered. People with healthy genes don't struggle with these illnesses. Why? The secret is in their DNA. They are wired and written differently from unhealthy people. It follows, therefore, that if we can synthetically replicate DNA that is healthy, and form

that into an active agent that will replicate those healthy
cells, we can rewire unhealthy DNA and breathe fresh life
into a broken species."

Reed took a deep sip of coffee and scanned the remainder of the article. It was a transcript from a talk Frank delivered to a research class in 2012.

Well, that doesn't sound at all like a mad scientist.

Another article was titled "Cancer: The Secret to Replicating Cells, by Dr. F. D. Morccelli."

So, Doc . . . you had a fascination with genetics. What did Mitch need to save you from?

The remaining articles were about various research projects. The most recent was dated twelve months before his death and detailed a special research grant from a medical company named Beaumont Pharmaceutical. For a research scientist, that seemed like another day at the office—certainly nothing that appeared murder-worthy.

If Frank was killed by the same people who were after Holiday, the link between them had to be the reason for their assassinations. But, assuming Morccelli's death six years before wasn't an accident, why wait this long to follow up with Holiday?

He was still in on it. Whatever's going on here, Holiday has been involved ever since. It's the only reason he would still be alive.

Reed sat back in his chair and rubbed his chin while staring at the screen. The reality of what he was looking at sank in slowly, then took hold of his mind. Oliver wasn't the villain here. Oliver was just another pawn. Somebody darker and bigger and lost in the shadows lay behind the curtain, calling the shots. They presumably killed Frank, and they now had reason to kill Holiday.

These people weren't killers, though. Criminals, for sure, but not hitmen. That's why they hired Oliver to get the job done, and Oliver passed the contract to Reed. When he realized that Reed had no intentions of continuing employment after his thirtieth kill, Oliver decided to set Reed up and have him thrown in prison for the Holiday murder.

There to die.

It hit Reed so hard he sat forward. Paul Choc, the Latino he killed in prison to secure his freedom. Was Choc another one of Oliver's henchmen who refused to continue employment? Somebody Oliver needed to be rid of?

This was a system. A machine for Oliver. Hire new people, run them until they quit, and then burn them. Only now, Oliver had lost control. He had failed to burn the Prosecutor, and whoever Oliver was hired by had turned elsewhere to finish the job. They had turned to The Wolf, this third-party assassin, and deployed him to destroy Reed by any means necessary.

Reed cleared the search history on the computer, then waved at a nearby barista and held up his phone. "Hey, do you have a charger for this?"

The kid pointed to a bank of wires along the far wall, then shuffled off without further comment. Reed jammed the charger into the phone, then leaned against the counter. If Holiday was in on it, he must have screwed up or outlived his usefulness. That would explain the sudden desire of the players behind the curtain to end his life. Either way, Reed was no longer comfortable leaving Banks with the drunken senator. He was probably harmless himself, but he was also a target, and not a very streetwise target at that. A cabin on the lake with an open wall full of windows was a dumb place to hide. A sniper of subpar skill could take out the senator from across the lake in broad daylight, and the FBI would have nothing to do about it. It was only a matter of time before Oliver, or whoever the hell was after Holiday, made another attempt. Banks needed to be gone before then. He would drive back to the lake and make arrangements to secure her somehow.

Reed closed the door of the coffee shop's restroom. It smelled like too much bleach sloshed at random over the tile floor. On his way to the urinal, he did a double-take of himself in the mirror. He looked like hell— messy hair and grime on his skin, and dark bags hanging under his bloodshot eyes.

This job is killing me, one way or the other.

"Welcome to Evan's." It was the sulky kid behind the counter.

"Thank you." The voice was clear and strong, late-twenties, brimming with confidence. "I'm Wolfgang."

Reed started, then zipped his pants as he stood in front of the urinal and waited.

Wolfgang. That's too much of a coincidence.

"I'm looking for my friend." Wolfgang spoke again, more casually this time.

Reed pictured the handsome man in the peacoat from the day before. Imagined him leaning against the counter, drumming his fingers on the tip jar, and shooting the cashier a wink.

"He's a big guy," Wolfgang said. "Brown hair. A real bad case of RBF."

Reed reached under his jacket and unholstered the pistol.

"He's in the restroom." The kid spoke without hesitation or interest.

Shit.

Reed press-checked his handgun and laid his finger on the trigger. Feet clicked on the hardwood floor, and somebody laughed.

"Great. Thanks, man."

"Hey, dude, what the—"

The kid's voice was broken off by the thunderous roar of a gun. The latch to the bathroom door exploded, sending shards of metal flying into the mirror as the door blew back on its hinges. Reed instinctively ducked as bullets tore through the wall just over his head, shaking the walls with each deafening clap.

With his hand cocked around the doorframe, Reed fired toward the attacker. The smaller-caliber handgun snapped like a popgun next to the bellow of whatever the hell was being fired at him.

Glass shattered, and the screams that ripped through the café were joined by the clatter of chairs colliding with tables. Reed pivoted around the door. Already swinging with his left fist, his knuckles connected with the metal slide of an enormous handgun just as The Wolf pulled the trigger again. The gunshot detonated, and the shock wave of the bullet passed by Reed's head as the muzzle flipped upward. Blood streamed from his ear, and every noise around him turned into ringing.

The man standing directly in front of him was of average height, just under six feet. His hair was close-cropped, and his eyes were crystal blue—deep and penetrating. He wore a black trench coat over a full suit —the same suit Reed had seen him in the day before outside the Mercedes. But the most striking thing about his appearance wasn't the suit, or the eyes, or even the oversized handgun he held. It was his smile. No, it wasn't a smile. It was a full-blown grin. And not the menacing, evil grin of a mob boss in a movie. This was more like the wild, unbridled grin of a kid with a new bike—pure, genuine joy.

Reed assimilated the entire scene in a millisecond and dismissed it all. He twisted his right hand and pressed the trigger of the Glock. It recoiled in his hand, and the bullet tore through the trench coat, just above the waistline, but he didn't hear the shot. The grin faded, and those crystal eyes flashed in pain. The man stumbled back, coughing and grabbing at his side as Reed followed the shot with a swift punch to the shoulder, knocking him farther back into the café. The gun clattered out of The Wolf's hand as he fell onto the floor, his face still awash with pain, but no blood seeped from the coat.

Body armor.

Reed kicked a chair out of the way and followed him, raising the Glock to align its sights with his forehead. He never got the chance to fire. The man on the floor twisted with blinding speed and swept his right leg against Reed's ankles. He stumbled to keep from falling, catching himself on the counter, but before he could adjust his aim, Wolfgang was already on his feet and spinning toward him. The grin was back, flashing at him a millisecond before a sweeping roundhouse kick knocked the Glock out of Reed's hand and sent his face crashing into the counter.

The room spun as Reed pushed himself up and snatched the Ka-Bar from underneath his shirt, then lunged toward The Wolf with an aggressive sweep of the blade. The man ducked and dodged the stroke with ease, then followed it with a rabbit punch to Reed's chest. The blow struck him with surprising force, knocking the wind out of his lungs and sending him stumbling backward.

"You don't disappoint, Montgomery. They told me you were good."

The Wolf reached into his pocket. A snapping sound rang out through the café, barely puncturing the ringing in Reed's ears. The bright outline of a switchblade knife glistened in The Wolf's right hand.

Reed steadied himself and adjusted his grip on the Ka-Bar, holding the weapon at shoulder height and keeping his eyes locked on his attacker. He spat blood. "I was a Marine."

"So I've heard."

"You know what the Marines say about knife fights?"

The Wolf grinned. "Let me guess . . . Don't get in one?"

"That's right. Because *everybody* gets hurt." Reed jumped a fallen chair and threw himself toward Wolfgang. He kicked up with his right foot, landing his boot into the man's knee as he swept the Ka-Bar toward his attacker's throat. The blade missed The Wolf's neck and tore into his jacket, shredding it and drawing blood from just above his body armor. The switchblade clattered to the floor a moment before they both followed, rolling onto the hardwood in a death lock. Reed fought to raise the knife still clutched in his right hand, but The Wolf's crushing grip closed around his wrist and kept tightening, squeezing the blood from his veins and paralyzing his fingers.

Reed rolled onto his back, and all he could see was The Wolf, leaning over him, his face still alive with that delighted grin. The knife's gleaming tip dangled inches from Reed's throat, and all at once, everything faded. He saw Banks's face again. The bright, honest smile. The way she touched his chest. Her gentle words and radiating warmth. It felt like home.

Home?

Wolfgang bore down on him, pushing, shoving, driving Reed's own knife closer to his jugular with every passing second.

I want to go home.

Wolfgang threw his shoulder into Reed's arm. The knife twitched, then fell half an inch closer.

22

R eed flailed out with his left arm, searching amid the table legs and spilled bagels. He back-handed a coffee mug and sent it spinning across the linoleum, then his fingers closed around something metallic—a spoon. He rammed the utensil into Wolf-gang's temple, digging through the skin and sending a stream of blood spurting over the floor. The Wolf shouted and released the pressure on the knife, crashing to the floor beside Reed. The Ka-Bar clattered down behind him, and Reed jumped to his feet, though he could barely see through the blood and adrenaline. As he searched for either gun on the floor, he heard The Wolf struggling to his feet behind him.

Reed grabbed the nearest chair and swung in a wide, powerful arc. The metal chair slammed into Wolfgang's upper arm, knocking the switchblade from his hand again and sending him crashing backward. Reed dropped the chair and dashed for the door, scrambling for the Land Rover keys in his pocket as he rushed into the parking lot. The all-too-familiar sound of sirens rang in the distance as he jerked the driver's door open and jumped inside.

Wolfgang appeared in front of the SUV, the giant handgun clutched between his fingers. He raised it, the grin returning as he laid his finger on the trigger. Reed ducked and shoved the vehicle into gear, slamming on the gas as the handgun thundered again. The bullet busted through the windshield as the tires bounced over the curb and the bumper collided with Wolfgang. Reed kept his head beneath the dash as he shifted into reverse and planted his foot into the accelerator again.

The big British motor rumbled, and the tires spun before catching on the frozen pavement and launching him backward. Reed sat up and turned the wheel to the right before slamming on the brake. The SUV slid into the street, the nose swinging around until he faced the oncoming lane of traffic. The top-heavy vehicle swayed as he completed the turn, and for a moment, he thought it would roll.

Reed threw the shifter back into drive and shoved the pedal to the floor, lurching the SUV forward in a screaming chorus of tires and swerving onto the main avenue of the tiny community. One headlight was out, and there was a big dent in the hood, but the Land Rover drove with surprising force. In mere seconds, the speedometer crossed sixty miles an hour as Reed turned around a tight corner, narrowly missing an oncoming police car. Blue lights blinded him, illuminating the inside of the SUV as bright as day. He jerked the wheel back to the left, sliding around the rear bumper of the squad car and redirecting the Land Rover down a new street.

Reed sucked in a deep breath and leaned back in the seat. His left arm stung and was soaked in blood. The interior of the SUV faded to dark as the lights of the town vanished over a hill. Reed checked the rearview mirror. No sign of The Wolf.

The split-second survey was almost a second too long. The Mercedes coupe spun out of a side street and into his path, leaving him just enough time to jerk the Land Rover toward the ditch and avoid a collision. A rattle of gunshots pounded over the wind, and the back glass exploded.

"Damn Uzi!" Reed pulled the wheel back to the left as the Land Rover bounced through a shallow ditch. Every time he tried to get back on the road, the front tires lost traction, and the Land Rover slid deeper into the ditch.

His search for the four-wheel-drive selector switch inside the console was futile, but just above the shifter was a silver label: FULL-TIME 4WD.

Let's see what you got.

Reed twisted the wheel to the right and redirected the SUV farther into the ditch. The tires locked on the mud, and the four-wheel-drive kicked in as the Land Rover hurtled out of the far side of the ditch and onto a city playground. A wooden tower next to a swing set exploded over the front bumper. Reed shouted and swerved to the right, barely missing a merry-go-round. Sand mixed with the snow, blasting into the air around all four corners of the SUV as bushes, playground equipment, and park benches were blown out of the way by the rampaging vehicle.

Reed hit the windshield wipers, and they bounced over the cracked glass, clearing his view to the edge of the park. He swerved around a picnic table and between two oak trees, then slammed on the brakes. The SUV slid to a halt, rocking on its heavy-duty springs as the back end swung around.

Stillness descended over the park. The hum of the engine was disrupted now by the irregular clicking of the damaged radiator fan. The hood was bucked upward, and steam rose from the engine bay, but the motor still rumbled.

Reed looked around, searching the far side of the park for any sign of the Mercedes. The Wolf hadn't followed him into the park, but his tracks were clear, marked by a war zone of broken playground parts and rutted snow. He wiped the sweat from his face and placed his hand on the shifter.

The Mercedes appeared to his right just as the cops showed up on his left, both cresting the hill outside the playground and driving toward him at different angles. Reed deliberated only an instant before turning away from the flashing blue and red lights. He couldn't kill the cops, but he was damn sure going to kill this Wolf.

Shoving the shifter back into drive, he planted his foot into the accelerator and turned toward the Mercedes. The four-wheel-drive locked in again, and the SUV hurtled over the railroad tie retainer of the playground before bouncing back onto the road. Each landing sent jarring shocks ripping through his spine, igniting fresh pain in his pounding head. He turned the nose of the Land Rover directly toward the Mercedes and stomped on the gas again. All four tires spun, and then the SUV sprang forward as though it were launched out of a catapult, rocketing directly down the middle of the two-lane road.

"Come on, bitch! Come get some!"

The speedometer passed seventy miles an hour as the space between them faded like ice in a skillet. The gleaming Mercedes logo hovered directly over the double yellow lines as The Wolf piloted his car down the middle of the road, straight for the Land Rover.

Reed tightened his fingers around the wheel. *I'll crush you.*

He heard the chatter of the Uzi first. Bullets slammed into the windshield and tore through the SUV's roof as The Wolf swung to the right at the last minute. A snap rang through the cabin as the front corner of the SUV's bumper collided with the Mercedes's side-view mirror, ripping it off. The silver coupe flashed past Reed without an inch to spare, leaving a rush of cold air and gasoline fumes in its wake.

Reed punched the steering wheel. He heard the squeal of tires behind him, then the sound of the coupe sliding around to give chase. He whipped the SUV off the street and back onto the state highway toward Lake Santeetlah.

"Come on, Wolf. Let's see if you run like you howl."

The accelerator bottomed out against the floor-board, and the speedometer rose—one hundred, then one twenty—as the wide, straight highway stretched out in front of him. The needle kept rising as the motor roared louder under the rattling hood. Reed tightened his fingers around the wheel and pushed his foot to the floor.

One forty-five. The motor capped out as the SUV seemed to hover over the asphalt, rushing past the mountains in a blur. He had pushed the Camaro well into the triple digits many times before, but this was an entirely different experience. With no snow tires or racing suspension to press him into the pavement, he stood one breath of a crosswind from being hurtled off the road to his imminent death.

Torrents of nervous sweat ran down his chest as he searched for the Mercedes. Nothing but darkness filled his mirrors, and he relaxed just a little off the pedal, letting the engine wind down a few octaves. Blazing through the rear glass and illuminating the SUV, the unmistakable Mercedes rocketed toward him as though it was powered by jet engines.

Reed jammed his foot into the accelerator again, negotiating around a gentle curve on the highway. The SUV rocked as though it were about to fly free of the pavement.

I'd give anything for my Camaro right now. This jerk would be history.

Reflective mile markers flashed past like Christmas lights as the Mercedes closed in on the Land Rover. The road began to rise and fall more aggressively, forcing both vehicles to decrease their speed, but leaving the clear advantage to the sport coupe. What had once been two hundred yards of buffer quickly shrank to twenty as The Wolf powered closer to the SUV. Any moment now, the chattering roar of the Uzi would open up again, slinging pounds of deadly lead through the back of the Land Rover and toward Reed's head.

Another curve appeared in the road, followed by a hill. Reed topped it first, followed by The Wolf a second behind. A piece of loose bodywork broke free of the Land Rover and flew over the roof. Something metallic clacked inside the engine bay, and a red light flashed next to the speedometer. With the radiator drained of coolant, the engine was starting to overheat.

Reed pressed the gas, sliding around a tighter corner of the road with almost too much momentum. The Land Rover slipped dangerously close to the edge of the highway before the tires caught and pulled him back to safety. The active four-wheel-drive was his only saving grace.

Another straightaway opened up a full hundred yards of flat pavement. The Mercedes was too quick. It lurched forward, closing the gap between them in seconds. He saw the driver's window slide down, followed a moment later by a hand clutching the small black submachine gun. Reed ducked and gripped the steering wheel, waiting for the burst of gunfire to tear through the back of his head.

Moments passed, and Reed looked back to see the Mercedes slowing behind him. The gap between them grew wider as the German coupe rolled to a full stop, now fifty yards back. No cops or anything in the road before them warranted the sudden stop. Behind him now were the bright red taillights of the Mercedes.

What the hell?

The realization hit Reed like a fist in the face. There could be only one reason The Wolf would cut him loose so suddenly—only one reason he would break off the chase.

Banks. God, no.

The SUV creaked and groaned as it shot forward into the darkness. The blast of the wind burned his eyes and chapped his skin as it howled through the open windshield, but he couldn't stop. He had to get back to the cabin.

_____

23

Lake Santeetlah, North Carolina

Smoke poured from the engine bay of the SUV as Reed rolled to a stop beside the cabin. Darkness hung over the A-frame like a blanket, thickened by a dense screen of fog that descended ahead of the coming storm. Reed slammed the door, circling the smashed front end of the Land Rover before pounding up the steps and into the cabin. The currents of tension that ruled his body made every motion feel overpowered and reckless, as though he were no longer controlling his own actions. The front door creaked on its hinges, and Reed searched the kitchen and dining room. Then he saw her.

"Chris!" Banks looked up from the couch, her eyes traveling over his disheveled clothes and bleeding arm. "My God! What happened?"

Reed motioned her toward the back of the cabin. "You have to get behind the wall. Where's Holiday?"

"He got drunk and went to bed. Chris, what's happening?"

"Come with me. Don't ask questions." They hurried into the master suite, the only room not fully exposed to the bank of windows covering the A-frame.

Reed hit the light switch. "Senator! On your feet!"

Holiday sat up on the bed, covering his ears and groaning. His face was pale and wrinkled into a deep frown. "Chris, what the hell? Get out of here!"

"Get up, Senator." Reed slammed the door shut and flipped the thumb latch.

Banks hurried past him and sat beside Holiday, patting him on the back. "Wake up, Uncle." Her voice was calm, reflecting her continued mental fortitude in the face of yet another wave of chaos.

Reed peered through the four-pane window at the empty woods outside, then pulled the curtains closed. "Do you have any weapons? Firearms?"

Holiday ran his hand over his face. "What are you talking about?"

"Guns, Senator. I need a gun."

Holiday shook his head as though Reed were speaking a different language, but he motioned toward the closet.

Reed jerked the door open and rifled through the clothes, digging past jackets and three-piece suits until he found a hard case nestled in the rear of the closet. A sinking feeling washed over him as the contents were exposed: a single, break-action shotgun. It was an over-under model, with fancy scrollwork carved into the walnut stock, and a frame inlaid with gold etching, tracing patterns down the receiver and toward the barrel.

"Is this it? Do you have a rifle?" Reed lifted the shotgun from the case and opened the breach. It was empty.

"That's all I have." Holiday glared at him. "What the hell is going on?"

Reed returned to the closet and dug into the darkness again. His hand landed on a paper box of twelve-gauge shells. As he read the label, his heart sank again.

Birdshot.

Reed slipped two shells into the open double chambers of the weapon, then slammed the breach closed before dumping the remainder of the box into his pants pocket. "They're coming for you, Senator. Right now."

The color drained from Holiday's face. "Who's coming?" His words slurred, spilling over one another as he tried to stand up.

Banks forced him back onto the bed.

"That's a damn good question. One I'd very much like you to answer. Who tried to kill you in Atlanta?"

Banks frowned at her uncle.

Holiday buried his face in his hands. "No. They can't get to me here. I have guards. The police. They're outside right now!"

Reed returned to the window, peering through a slit in the curtain. "The police can't save you, Senator. Maybe I can, but you need to start talking. Who wants you dead?"

Holiday shook his head again, more adamantly this

time. "No. I'm not talking to you about this. I don't know who the hell you think you are, but—"

"Don't test me, Senator!" Reed barked into Holiday's face, grabbing him by the shoulder and shaking him.

The senator's head rolled back, and his mouth fell open. His memory, once fogged with confusion and intoxication, suddenly cleared. "You. . . . It's *you!*"

Reed cursed under his breath and took a step back. He should have seen this coming. How many times had the tired Senator told Reed he looked familiar? The cat was out of the bag now.

"You kidnapped me! You beat me in that trailer! *'Don't test me.'* That's what you said to me then!"

Holiday dove toward him, and Reed turned with a quick twist of his hips, raising his fist and driving it straight into Holiday's temple with the full force of a left-cross. The senator's assault stopped mid-strike, his eyes rolled back in his head, and he crumbled to the ground without a sound.

Banks gasped and jumped from the bed. "Chris! What the hell! What are you doing?" Her voice cracked with emotion and panic.

A sudden thud resonated through the window, followed almost immediately by a cry of pain, and then the unmistakable sound of metal slicing through flesh.

Reed shouldered the shotgun and hurried into the living room. "Stay here. Lock the door!"

The words had barely left his lips before a loud pop rang out through the cabin, and the power went out.

They're here.

Reed whispered this time. "Shut the door. Don't come out for anyone."

He heard Banks turn the lock behind him as he slipped across the living room. The front door swung open and the hinges groaned again. In the distance, the lake lapped against the shore, while trees creaked and rustled. Reed waited for a moment, listening for any sign of the guards pacing outside, waiting and hoping for a reassuring shout from someplace in the shadows. Nothing. With the shotgun lifted, he stepped out onto the porch, adjusting his vision to the inky darkness. Nervous tension commanded every inch of his body. He had no idea what he was walking into or how many men waited in the darkness. The Wolf could be one of them, or maybe an army of goons wielding submachine guns stood amongst the trees. There was no way to know—no way to prepare.

Where are you?

His boots sank in the loose snow as he moved away from the cabin. Each step was measured and slow, bouncing back and forth between the shadows like a lynx on the hunt.

The first guard lay face-up, his throat sliced ear-to-ear. Both his sidearm and rifle were gone, leaving nothing but a growing patch of scarlet snow and a corpse already stiffening in the sub-freezing tempera-ture. Reed cursed and moved away from the body, sinking deeper into the shadows. A faint outline of footprints led away from the corpse, toward the lake, but they were rapidly filling as the snowfall returned, drifting down between the trees in a thickening cloud.

Dry chills ripped through his chest, and his fingers tingled around the stock of the shotgun, turning red as he tightened his grip. The trees around him were conspicuously silent of the forest sounds he had become accustomed to—the scampering of a squirrel, the hoot of an owl. Only the wind and the creek of the trees broke the stillness, each step bringing him closer to the lake and deeper into the shadows.

A scream ripped through the forest. Loud and long, then cut short. It was a man's scream—another one of the guards. Reed jerked the shotgun to his shoulder and spun around. The muzzle rose and fell with each breath, and once again the forest fell into deathly stillness.

Where are you?

Reed crept back toward the cabin. Slipping behind a tall red oak, he knelt in the dirt, watching the A-frame through narrowed eyes.

There.

It wasn't movement or even the sound of a twig breaking in the stillness. It was a shadow with a hard outline—too hard and defined to be natural—huddled behind a bush twenty yards away. Reed held the shotgun just below his eye line and faded between the trees like an apparition. Each footfall was slow and deliberate, minimizing the sound of collapsing snow. The wind picked up around him, howling through the trees, as he moved another ten feet around the back of the bush and toward the man on the other side.

He pivoted the muzzle of the shotgun around the bush, coming to rest on a body lying on the other side.

The second guard lay on his back, his throat torn open, and his vacant eyes filled with death.

The realization hit Reed a moment too late. He turned and ducked, but couldn't avoid the blow to the back of his neck with the force of a baseball bat, knocking him to his knees and sending the shotgun tumbling from his fingers. Reed hit the ground and rolled to the left, twisting his body to avoid the next blow. Bone cracked as something hard and cold collided with his shin, and the pain that rippled through Reed's leg was almost as powerful as the fear that dominated his mind.

A mountain of a man leaned over him—a full seven feet tall, with gargantuan hands, gripping a four-foot metal pipe. The moment their eyes met Reed's heart skipped a beat. The big man grinned with gapped teeth. One eye stared at Reed while the other wandered at random, gazing into the forest.

The goon from prison. Did he work for Oliver all along?

His thick lips sneered down at Reed as he swung again, straight for Reed's chest. Reed rolled to the left, and the metal pole slammed into his hip with bone-crushing force, igniting pain that shot down his leg and flooded his brain.

The shotgun. Where's the shotgun?

Reed clawed at the dirt and swept his arm through the low piles of loose snow. He fought to pull himself backward, then felt the smooth metal of the double-barrel shotgun beneath his fingers. Before he could snatch it up, he saw the glint of the pole arcing through the air toward him. He rolled, and the weapon glanced off his shoulder.

No. I'm not dying this way!

Reed lifted the gun and swung the muzzle toward the giant's torso. The big man was already mid-swing when Reed pressed both triggers, dumping two twelve-gauge shells directly into his chest. The thunder of the shotgun shook the forest as the birdshot tore into the man and launched him backward.

Reed snapped the breach open and dug fresh shells out of his pocket, slammed them into the dual chambers, and flicked it shut again. The snowfall that swirled around him assumed the shape of a vortex, mixing with the wind and tearing at his hair. He spun back toward the forest and raised the shotgun. Twenty yards away, circling between the tree trunks, a shadow ran away from him, deeper into the woods.

The shotgun boomed like a cannon, and Reed dumped the empty shells and replaced them, breaking into a jog toward the elusive shadow. Blinding rage and the will to destroy overcame his awareness of the world around him, creating a tunnel that led to his next target.

The shadow faded into the forest. Reed swept the shotgun through the trees, searching for the outline of the running man. He was gone, swallowed by the storm.

Reed lowered the weapon and sucked in a breath. Only the whistle of the wind joined him in the forest now. Everything else was cold and empty. Why was life always a vapor between his fingers?

As he turned back toward the cabin, a dull orange lit the forest on the far side of the howling curtain of snow. A leaden weight descended into his stomach as he began to run again, crossing ditches and ducking under trees. As the yards passed under his feet, the orange glow clarified, joined by a trace of warmth.

The cabin was engulfed in flames.

24

Tall columns of smoke poured from the metal roof as fire consumed the log walls, filling the front porch. Glass shattered and a window frame collapsed. The Land Rover was also on fire, blazing beside the cabin with oily smoke clouding over the engine bay.

"Banks!" Reed dashed for the front door, but an overwhelming surge of heat stopped him in his tracks. He screamed into the fire. "*Banks!*"

"She's right here, Reed!" The voice carried over the wind behind him. Strong. Defiant. Just a hint of a British accent.

Reed spun and jerked the shotgun to his shoulder, aiming it at Oliver Enfield, his former employer, long-time mentor, and personal Judas. Banks was pinned under his left arm, standing on her toes as Oliver held a polished 1911 pistol to her temple. Just beside them, Holiday knelt on the ground with his hands in the snow and his head bowed as the giant pointed a massive revolver at the back of his skull. The big man's shirt was shredded from the shotgun blast, revealing the battered and torn surface of a Kevlar vest beneath it. His good eye glowed with devilish glee as actual drool dripped from his lip.

Reed slowly lowered the shotgun, keeping his fingers on the dual triggers of the weapon as he walked down the hillside, stopping twenty feet away.

Oliver grinned. His bald head shone in the dancing light of the flames, gleaming over a row of perfect white teeth. Tears streamed down Banks's face as she gasped for breath under the suffocating grip.

"Well, Reed, you found me. You here to pay for my cabin?"

Reed switched his gaze from the tall killer, to Banks, to Holiday kneeling in the snow. "Let her go."

Oliver laughed. "Who? This bitch? You know, I've hired a lot of military washouts, Reed, but I miscalculated with you. I thought somebody who gunned down half a dozen military contractors must be a coldhearted killer, but what I failed to appreciate was the *why* of it all. You're just a little superman, aren't you? Always looking out for the little guy."

Without blinking, and with a mind dulled beyond any perception of precise emotion, Reed stared at Oliver. He felt angry, yes, but more than that, he felt cold. For three years he surrendered his soul to this man, traveling around the world to gun down whoever he was told to kill. He never questioned. Never objected. He accepted the reality as his job, and he accepted Oliver as his boss—a man to obey, if not to trust. That had been the worst decision Reed ever made, not because it resulted in his ultimate betrayal, but because it ended here. In the snow. With Banks's life hanging in the balance.

Oliver jerked Banks's hair back, exposing her neck. "Tell me, girl. Who did he say he was? Let me guess . . . a *venture capitalist.*"

Confusion and hurt poured into her soul as she looked at Reed and then squeezed her eyes shut. That pained look of desperation and fear tore Reed to his very core, shattering every confidence and justification he ever had, stripping him all the way to the foundation of who he really was: a heartless killer. A man who had sold his soul.

Oliver laughed. "Of course he did. That's what I trained him to say. I mean, he can't walk around bragging about being a cold-blooded murderer, can he?"

Holiday's eyes were still clouded with drunkenness, but there was a clarity that burned through the fog—a single point of focus strong enough to draw Reed's attention. "Did you kill him?" Holiday asked.

The years of pain and insecurity and whatever horrible secrets Holiday bore wore down his tired features, making him look years older than he was. The circles under his eyes were darker and heavier than before, and he sagged in total defeat. But Reed could still see him clinging to this one point of tension—the burden Holiday had carried ever since his best friend had been murdered in New Orleans. The guilt that Holiday himself was responsible.

"No." Reed met his tired gaze with all the honesty

and integrity he had left in his blackened soul. Holiday nodded once, and Reed turned back to his old mentor. "*Paul Choc.*"

Oliver tilted his head, feigning confusion, then he laughed. "Oh, you mean Blazer. The man you killed."

"He was one of yours, wasn't he? A contractor you needed to burn."

"Killer in, killer out, Reed. It was his choice to walk away from me, just like it was yours. And he paid for it, just like you will."

Reed spat the remnants of blood from his mouth. "Okay. Well, I'm here. What do you want?"

Oliver grinned. "Thirty lives, Reed. I want you to finish your job."

Reed's fingers tightened around the grip of the gun, the barrel hovered at waist-height, pointing at the gut of the cross-eyed man. Through bared teeth, he hissed, "*Let her go.*"

Oliver's grin perished, and he jammed the gun deeper into her temple, pressing until Banks cried out in pain. Streams of tears ran down her face.

"Do it, Reed. Finish your job!"

The senator looked at Reed with steady, unblinking eyes, and slowly, Reed dropped the barrel of the shotgun over the groin of the giant, over Holiday's face, and then centered it on his chest.

"Don't. . . . Please don't do it." Banks sobbed, her neck twisted as Oliver drove her head into his shoulder with the pressure of the pistol.

"Pull the trigger, Reed, or I'll pull mine!" Oliver's expression reignited into a vicious smirk.

The desperate pleading in Banks's eyes tore straight through Reed's heart like a rifle bullet, making him go weak at the knees. The snowflakes that fell against her elegant features faded quickly to raindrops as thunder echoed overhead. She looked so perfect, even with the pain that dominated her face. She looked like everything he never knew he always wanted.

Oliver jerked upward, lifting Banks off her feet by her neck as she choked and scratched at his arm. *"Do it, Reed!"*

The senator still stared at Reed, but a calm settled over his tired eyes. He nodded once. "Save my goddaughter."

The giant cursed, his guttural voice booming over the wind. He jammed the barrel of the massive revolver into Holiday's back and pushed him forward onto his hands and knees, his head bowed directly beneath the twin muzzles of the shotgun.

Reed settled the butt of the weapon into his shoulder and stared down the barrel at Holiday's forehead. He placed his index finger over the front trigger and closed his left eye, then drew in a deep breath.

Banks fought against Oliver's grip and reached out for her godfather. "Please . . . don't . . ."

"It's okay, Banks." Holiday's voice was soft. "I love you."

Holiday's left hand twitched, and his palms settled into the slurry of snow and mud. His left index finger rose and tapped down. Once. Twice.

On the third tap, Reed spun to the left at the same moment Holiday launched himself to his feet. The revolver barked, and the shotgun spun upward, still swinging to the left as Reed depressed the trigger. The world around Reed descended into a chaos of slow motion. Blood exploded from Holiday's back, knocking him to his knees even as the senator fought to turn and assault the giant. The shotgun recoiled, spitting a deadly spray of lead birdshot over Oliver's right shoulder, inches from Banks's head. The edge of the shot pattern caught the right side of Oliver's face, shredding the skin and flesh from his cheek and neck. The kingpin killer screamed and fell back, dropping the handgun and releasing Banks. He clawed at his face, shrieking as though he were on fire.

Reed redirected the shotgun and depressed the second trigger. The back of the giant's head vanished into a blast of hair and brain matter as he crumbled to the ground. Reed snapped the breach open as he stepped over Holiday and toward Oliver, ejecting empty shells over his arm. He dug into his pocket for the next load, grabbed two shells, and lifted them toward the breach.

Oliver's face was a clouded, distorted mess of flesh and bone. His right eye was gone, and a bloody socket was left behind. He launched himself forward with unprecedented ferocity, grabbing the shotgun and jerking Reed off balance. They crashed to the ground as blows rained down on Reed's exposed face. The fresh shells slipped from his fingers and he released the shotgun as they tumbled through the snow.

Reed's fingers closed around Oliver's arms, and he dug in, channeling all of his strength and anger into this moment. This man had become the monster in his closet—a lying, thieving conniver who dangled freedom in front of his nose then snatched it away at the last moment. He would rip Oliver limb from limb before he walked away.

A knife flashed, clenched between Oliver's white fingers. It sliced through Reed's shirt, leaving a gushing red line behind it. Reed screamed, hurled Oliver off of him, and drove his left fist into Oliver's stomach. The slick mud gave way beneath him as he followed up the punch, and Reed fell forward over Oliver as both men rolled down the steep lake bank. Icy water closed over Reed's head as the knife flashed again and dug into his side. Oliver landed on his stomach, pressing him deeper into the water and pinning him against the mud.

Reed couldn't breathe. Darkness closed overhead. The knife dug into his shoulder and stuck there as Oliver's big hands closed around his throat and slammed the back of his head into the muddy lake bottom. Reed kicked and struggled, clawing for any leverage to shove his attacker off. His fingers dug through the mud for a rock or a stick, but nothing except the slimy lake bottom touched his fingers as life slipped from his lungs. Oliver bellowed, pushing Reed deeper into the mud. Each heartbeat that pounded through his skull came slower than the one before as death encroached on his consciousness.

The thunder of the shotgun rang out from the edge of Reed's reality, and a rippling shockwave shot through Reed's body as Oliver fell forward. The mutilated features of the killer crashed into the lake. The iron grip loosened around his throat, and Reed launched himself out of the water, gasping as he cleared the surface. Oliver flopped and screamed on top of him, but the power from his body was gone.

On the shore, Banks stood in the pouring rain with the shotgun in her trembling hands. Tears streamed down as she stared at Reed, full of so much pain and sadness. In an instant, that stare communicated all of the anger, hurt, and agony of the betrayal she felt. All of it directed at him.

Reed met her gaze and shoved Oliver back, then reached out for her. "Banks! Wait!"

She dropped the shotgun and shook her head once. "Don't go!"

Water splashed around him as Reed fought to his knees.

"Banks!"

She ran up the hill, vanishing into the rain and darkness, and leaving him in the shallows. Reed screamed into the howling wind, feeling his throat choked by cold and emotion and so much pain. His hands trembled and he started to slog out of the lake, but she was gone. In that split moment, the woman he loved slipped away like water between his fingers.

Reed's fingers closed around his limp mentor's arms and he hoisted him out of the water and hurled him onto the bank. The effort almost exhausted him as ripples of agony swept down his arms from his shoulder, mixing with blood and lake water. But he didn't stop.

The old killer landed on the bank with a grunt and looked up at him through a single bloodshot eye. His entire right cheek was gone, exposing missing teeth and a shredded ear. A tongue covered in blood lapped against the roof of his mouth as his torn lips lifted into a twisted grin. "Look at you . . . saved by a bitch."

Reed retrieved Oliver's fallen knife and slammed it into his stomach, digging in and twisting. Oliver's head lifted off the bank as a scream ripped free of his mutilated throat. He coughed up blood, spraying it over Reed's chest before his head slammed back into the bank again. Reed shoved the knife in deeper, pushing it until it slammed into Oliver's spine.

"Who are they, Oliver?" Reed screamed over the rain, bellowing right into Oliver's face.

Oliver spat, then gasped for air. The sound rasped and choked as blood puddled in his throat. "Don't you wish . . . you knew?"

Reed screamed again and drove his fist into what remained of the old killer's face. "Tell me, Oliver! Who are they? Who ordered the Holiday hit?"

Oliver rasped for air, his roving eye settling on Reed. Calm fell over the pain, and his torn lips twisted into a slight smile. "Maybe . . . you should ask . . . Kelly."

Without another breath, his head fell back against the mud, and the life vanished from his body.

Reed jerked the knife free and threw his head back, screaming into the rain. Rage and unbridled madness overtook him, and he jumped up and drove his foot into Oliver's ribcage, but the old man already lay still and lifeless—as dead as the hundreds of men and women who died under his command.

Reed turned away from the fallen killer and scanned the hillside, screaming again for Banks. Only the rain answered his cries, mixed with a cough and a soft voice from farther away from the water. Reed fought his way up the bank and followed the sound, running through the mud and staggering amongst the trees.

The voice came from the far side of the giant's body. Reed slid to his knees and lifted Holiday's head. The senator blinked once as he stared at Reed and then smiled softly. "Damn . . . venture capitalists . . ."

"Senator, you're dying. I need you to talk to me. Who wanted you dead?"

Holiday coughed up fresh pools of blood, and he shook with a violent tremor. Then he closed his eyes.

"Senator! Talk to me!"

Holiday's lips twitched, and Reed leaned down, pressing his ear close to the senator's mouth.

"*From end . . . to end.*"

"From end to end? I don't know what that means!"

Holiday's neck went limp, and his head rolled back. Reed laid him down, then stood up slowly. He looked down at the dead senator, then back at the bloodied, crushed body of his mentor. Of all the gory scenes of carnage he had experienced in his life, this one gripped him more deeply. It sank into his heart and enflamed anger like he had never felt before.

Oliver's last words echoed in his tired mind. "*Maybe you should ask Kelly.*"

Panic pushed back his anger as the reality sank in. Reed fell to his knees again and rolled the giant over. The big man's face was gone, and his jacket fell open. Reed searched the pockets, dumping out wads of gum wrappers and a pocketknife, and then his fingers hit something hard and heavy. As he pulled it out, the light from the distant cabin fire glinted off polished metal. It was an aluminum card about the size of a credit card, painted black with nothing but a single image etched on one side: a silver badger. Reed shoved it into his pocket, then resumed his search until he found a pair of car keys with a Cadillac logo emblazoned on them. He snatched up the massive revolver lying in the mud beside the body, and turning toward the hill, he broke into a run.

25

Reed found the Escalade parked a hundred yards behind the cabin on the side of the road. He slammed it into gear and shoved the accelerator to the floor, spinning the big SUV around and back onto the road. He swerved past oncoming police cars as he wound his way through the mountains, topping hills and crashing through canyons.

Blood streamed from his arm. He tore off a shred of his shirt and jammed it into the knife wound, maintaining pressure on the wad of dirty cloth as he crossed out of the lake town and blew through Robbinsville. Everything fogged around him, blurring almost out of view. It was all he could do to keep the SUV pointed straight down the road, but he didn't relax on the speed. Only one thought pounded through his skull: *Please let her be alive.*

The one hundred twenty miles back to northern Atlanta blazed by him in ninety minutes, swirling into a series of highways and small towns that were more like a memory than an experience. As he crashed into the outskirts of Canton, he could already see an orange light in the back of the neighborhood and the column of smoke that blackened the sky.

Reed screeched around a corner on the narrow residential streets and slammed on the brakes. He left the revolver in the passenger seat and jumped out, still holding the shirt against his wound as he raced the last few yards down the street. Fire trucks lined the sidewalks, blocking his view as dirty, tired firemen walked back and forth between them. He pressed through the crowd, ignoring several shouts for him to stop as he slid around the last truck and faced the house at the end of the cul-de-sac.

Nothing remained of the home. Black ashes were soaked but still smoldering at the bottom of fallen brick walls and the remnants of a pine wood frame. Firemen lined the edge of the lot, showering the foundation with streams of pressurized water, but it wasn't necessary—the flames were gone, leaving only charred emptiness behind.

Three men in white plastic suits stood by two stretchers near a white van marked *"County Coroner."* Reed stumbled toward the stretchers, his hands hanging limp at his sides. The ache of irrefutable reality sank into his soul as he shoved the first man aside and stared down at the small, charred body on the first stretcher. He collapsed to his knees, tears gushing from his eyes as he fell forward. He couldn't feel the hands on his shoulders or the ground beneath his legs. Racking pain ripped through his body, starting at his throat and burning through his stomach.

"Sir . . . you need to stand up. Come with me." The cop's eyes were filled with compassion as his firm but gentle grip descended on Reed's arm. "Sir, stand up, please. We'll get you help."

Reed watched the stretchers as they vanished inside the van. The last glimpse of the bodies faded inside, and the doors crashed shut.

"Can you tell us who they were? We haven't identified the bodies."

Reed forced back the tears and ran his tongue over dry lips. He closed his eyes and bowed his head. When he spoke, he didn't recognize his own voice. The toneless words sounded as though they came from another world. Another man. "Her name is Kelly Armstrong."

"Thank you. I'm so sorry." The officer patted his arm. "Come with me. You need medical attention."

A soft whimpering rang from beyond the fire engines. Reed's eyes snapped open, and he looked back toward the burned-out house. He heard it again—barely audible but strong.

"Baxter?"

Reed pushed past the policeman, around the firefighters, and through the rubble of the house toward the burned-out backyard. He heard the whimper again —stronger this time. He grabbed a picnic table half-consumed by the scalding flames, and pain shot up his arms as the embers of the dying fire burned into his skin. With one powerful push, he threw it back and looked down.

Baxter's short brown hair was singed from the fire, and his big black eyes were bloodshot as he stared up at Reed. Swollen red burn marks crisscrossed his skin, and his breaths came in short, whistling bursts. He lay on the ground, barely moving, his paws and legs blackened by ashes and soot.

Reed scooped the big dog up, holding him close to his chest as tears streamed down his cheeks. "It's okay, boy. I'm here. I've got you."

The bulldog whimpered again and pressed his wrinkly face close to Reed's chest. He smelled of ashes and smoke, and his skin trembled when Reed touched the burn marks, but he didn't fight as he settled into Reed's arms.

Reed turned back to the street but stopped as he saw the officer step forward, his head tilted toward the radio clipped to his uniform. The cop nodded once, then reached for his gun. "Sir, stop where you are. Put down the dog."

Reed didn't wait for the gun to rise from the holster. He dashed back through the ashes of the home, slipping through the backyard as men shouted behind him. With Baxter clutched in his arms, he ran through the yards of half a dozen homes before dashing between two houses and reaching the Escalade.

Shouts and sirens rang out, but Reed ignored them as he swept the revolver aside and set Baxter into the passenger seat. The tires spun, and the SUV slid around again, back toward the open street. Sirens faded behind him, wisping away as quickly and elusively as the smoke into the black sky.

Reed didn't try to hold back the sobs that racked his body. His arms shook as the tears streamed down his face. He could still see her small, burned body lying on that stretcher. Faceless. Nameless. Her unborn baby inside of her. The reality that it was *his* fault was inescapable. He had brought Kelly into this and made her fiancé and her innocent baby victims of his own failures. And these people, these shadows behind the curtain, these demons who called the shots, held Oliver on a leash, and released murderers into the world—he didn't know what they were protecting or why, but it was obvious they would stop at nothing to get what they wanted.

Baxter sat up in the passenger seat, his beady eyes fixed on the bloody revolver lying on the floorboard. His lip curled up over his jutting teeth as his chest rumbled into a deep, menacing growl. Reed placed one hand on the big dog, sinking his fingers into the singed hair and soft skin.

There was nobody left—no allies, no friends. Banks was gone. Holiday was dead. Winter had cut Reed off. There was only one choice before him—only one road to travel. He blinked back the tears and clenched his fingers around the wheel.

"Don't worry, boy. We're going to kill them. We're going to kill them all."

Want to find out what happened in Iraq?

Read *Sandbox*, the Reed Montgomery prequel for FREE.

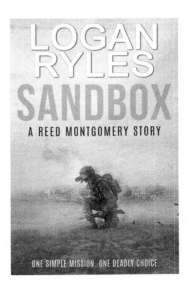

Visit join.loganryles.com/reed-begins to download your free copy.

THE STORY CONTINUES WITH...

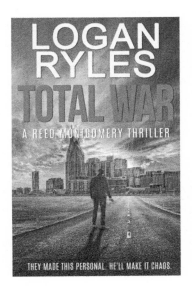

Turn the page to read the first chapter.

TOTAL WAR

REED MONTGOMERY BOOK 3

**Atlantic City,
New Jersey**

"Are you here to check in?"

The woman behind the counter wore a red velvet vest, black satin pants, and shoes that gleamed under the casino lights. Her hair was knotted behind her head, exposing the tight skin of too many facelifts and not enough vitamin D. The smile she wore couldn't hide the exhaustion in her eyes or the disinterest in her tone.

Reed pushed his aviator sunglasses closer to his eyes. He laid the metal business card on the counter, and the casino lights glinted off its glossy black surface, shining on the emblem of a silver badger etched in the center of the card.

"I'm here to see Mr. Muri."

A shadow of emotion broke the exhaustion in her vacant gaze. Or maybe it was excitement. Trepidation?

They so often look the same. I wonder if she knows what kind of man she works for.

The woman smiled again, nodded once, and disappeared through a doorway. Reed replaced the card into his pocket and leaned against the counter. The edge of the granite bit into the back of his sport coat, colliding with his bruised back. Through the dark lenses of his sunglasses, the flashing neon lights were only partially muted. The *shrink* of slot machine levers melded with the clinking ring of the dials as they spun like Ferris wheels on crack. A craps table on the far side of the room was crowded by a dozen men in collared shirts, half-drunk, leaning in and shouting as the dice bounced over the scarlet felt. The faint odor of flowers wafted from an air freshening device buried in the vents of the overhead AC unit, a clever design that subdued the chaos and tension of the room and further facilitated reckless spending.

What a masterpiece. And people wonder why the house always wins.

"Sir?" The woman returned to the counter.

Reed stood up with a soft grunt as his aching muscles objected to the movement. Her smile was gone now. Two large men with emotionless stares accompanied her, both dressed in dark grey suits that bulged around oversized arms and barrel chests.

Why do all mob goons look the same?

"These men will escort you to Mr. Muri."

Reed stepped around the counter. The first goon pushed the door open and led the way into a hall while the second fell in behind Reed. Flashes of orange and blue from the casino floor vanished into a sterile white of LED overheads glaring onto the floor and walls. The hall reminded Reed of a sick ward in a hospital—bare minimum in every way with plain metal doors and cheap linoleum flooring.

The house doesn't waste money, either. Another reason it always wins.

Except for today. Today, everyone would lose. It was why Reed left Georgia and drove twelve hours to be there. It was why he jacked himself up on caffeine pills before leaving the rental car in an alley and slipping up to the casino like another drunk tourist—casual, but fully alert and ready to kill.

Today the house will burn.

Twin silver doors blocked their path at the end of the hall. The lead goon punched a button on the wall, and the elevator opened immediately, revealing an interior decorated with mahogany panels and gold rails. Gentle elevator music drifted down from invisible speakers. Reed walked in and waited while the two men swiped ID cards. The doors glided shut, and they turned on him as the car began to descend.

"Arms up." The command was as blunt and bland as the man who grunted it. Reed lifted his arms while the men felt down his legs, around his waist, and over his ribcage. The big hand running up his side stopped at the suede holster with the oversized revolver tucked inside. The retainer strap clicked, and the weapon fell into the goon's fingers.

The men looked down at the massive handgun. Even with a short, four-inch barrel, the .500 magnum revolver dwarfed their large hands. As the first man lifted the gun and raised both eyebrows, the gaping, .50 caliber muzzle stared Reed in the face

Reed shrugged. "Bear hunting."

They sneered at him, and the revolver disappeared beneath one man's sport coat as the elevator bell rang and the doors rolled open. Reed was shoved forward into a hallway that couldn't have been more different from the stark white of four floors above. More mahogany panels framed dark red carpet, gold trim, and brass light fixtures. Shadows clung to the corners, and the big feet of the two men behind him barely made a sound as they propelled him down the hallway toward the tall oak door at the end. Both men placed their thumbs against a black panel mounted next to the doorjamb, and the lock clicked.

This Muri guy really thinks he's something. All middlemen do.

The door swung open without a sound, and once more, the meaty hands pushed him forward. Reed stumbled across the carpet onto a thick rug, his vision temporarily blinded by the flash of lights overhead. Built into the walls of the large room were tall book-shelves, and a giant leather couch faced him next to a glass table stacked with liquor bottles. A quick survey of the occupants revealed a tall, thin man in a suit standing in one corner, a whiskey glass in one hand and his black hair plastered against his scalp. Only one other person occupied the parlor, and he faced Reed from the comfort of the oversized leather couch, one leg crossed over the other and round glasses mounted over a pointed nose. His face was worn and pale, with a network of scars tracing his left cheek and leading up to his ear.

Reed heard the door click behind him, and he tugged at the bottom of his jacket, brushing out the wrinkles left by the thick fingers of the two goons. One thug handed the revolver to the man on the couch, who surveyed the weapon, then motioned toward a chair sitting across from him. Reed adjusted his sunglasses again, then took a seat.

"Welcome." The man's voice was smooth, laden with a thick Swiss accent, but he spoke with the relaxed tone of a person comfortable with English. "Charles, won't you pour our guest a brandy?"

The tall man with the black hair lifted a bottle of brown liquor, then handed Reed a tumbler textured with diamond stipples. The first sip revealed the unmistakable smoky smoothness of a high-dollar brand—something old and rare.

"Thank you." Reed lifted the glass toward the man on the couch and was answered with a slight bow.

"Whom do I have the pleasure of hosting?" The voice was still calm, but an air of directness slipped into the tone.

Reed set the glass on the table and popped his knuckles. "Call me Chris. It's not overly important who I am."

The man shrugged—slight and disinterested. "Fine. What can I do for you, *Chris?*"

"I understand you're in the business of brokering contractors. Specifically, the criminal kind."

The room fell silent. Reed was vaguely aware of the two big men standing to his left, and Charles stepped behind a tall armchair, his hands falling out of sight.

Probably to a gun or a knife. As if either will save him.

The man on the couch smiled. "You're quite mistaken. I'm a simple businessman. A casino owner. Nothing more."

Reed leaned back in the chair and crossed his legs. He flipped the card from his pocket and onto the coffee table between them, then returned the smile. "No, you're not. You're Cedric Muri. The goon broker."

The smile on Cedric's face faded as he eyed the card with the glowing silver badger. He took a long sip of brandy, then returned his gaze to Reed. "Where did you get that?"

"From a dead man. Big fellow, cross-eyed. Carried a rather large Smith & Wesson revolver. The one you're holding, as it happens."

Cedric's gaze fell to the weapon, then returned to Reed. Fire blazed in his eyes, and he dropped the brandy onto the coffee table. He sat forward. "Why are you here?"

"We'll get to that in just a moment. First, I need some information. Besides the big guy I killed in North Carolina, you also hired out some East European thugs to a South American prick named Salvador. While I was busy carving them up in Atlanta, one of them mentioned your name. So, my question is, why are you supplying soldiers to the people who want to kill me?"

Cedric's lips lifted into a smile. "Reed Montgomery. The assassin."

Reed nodded. "That's me, although I'm trying my damnedest to retire. People like you are making it difficult."

"That's because people like me are threatened by rogue assassins like you."

"You wouldn't be if you had stayed out of it. Those two Europeans I mentioned kidnapped a young lady on behalf of Mr. Salvador. I happen to like her a lot. And then, of course, there are the men I gunned down at Pratt-Pullman Yard in Atlanta. None of these shitheads were proper soldiers. None of them were Oliver Enfield's men. So they must've been yours, and you're going to tell me who paid for them."

Cedric drummed the tips of his fingers against each other, producing the only noise in the still room. He lifted one finger and motioned toward Reed. "I think we're done here, Mr. Montgomery. I'm sure Mr. Salvador will pay handsomely for your head."

Reed lifted the brandy glass and drained the contents. "I was hoping you'd say that."

The floor creaked under the weight of one of the big men, whose reflection Reed saw flash in the gold railing behind Cedric. As he leaned forward to deliver a death blow, Reed sprang from the chair, and without turning around, grabbed him by the arm. With a quick heave, he bent forward and dragged him over his back. The goon sailed over the chair and crashed against the tabletop in an explosion of glass. A gunshot cracked from behind Reed, snapping against the wooden walls and reverberating in his ears. Cedric dove to the carpet as Reed followed him, and Charles vanished behind the minibar.

The revolver's grip filled Reed's hands as he jerked it off the floor and spun it toward the thug lying amid the shattered table. With a quick pull of the trigger, the room erupted into an explosion. The man on the floor convulsed as his head was blasted apart under the smashing impact of the 350-grain projectile. The shock-wave that tore through Reed's arm sent him hurtling back against the floor as though a horse had kicked him. Glass tore through his jacket and into his shoulder, sinking into flesh so bruised he barely felt the cuts. Reed redirected the revolver and fired again, sending the second goon crashing to the floor.

Two more shots tore through the paneling that sheltered Charles, sending shards of wood spraying over the floor amid the broken liquor bottles. The gunshots ceased. Reed picked himself up, rubbing a sore shoulder. The handgun kicked like nothing he'd ever fired before. His hand ached, and his ears rang from the thunderous blast.

But it damn sure gets the job done.

The two fallen gunmen lay still and silent, with none of the twitches or residual fighting power he was used to men having after he shot them in the chest with his 9mm. The Smith & Wesson 500 was the cannon of the handgun world. The last word.

A gasping, rasping sound leaked from behind the couch. Reed rubbed his thumb against the Smith and shoved the couch out of the way, exposing the groveling figure of Cedric Muri on the floor behind it. Slobber and spilled brandy coated the hardwood floor beneath him, and he scrambled backward as Reed advanced.

"You should've worked with me, Cedric."

"Please . . ." Cedric held out his hand. "Let's discuss this!"

Reed squatted on the carpet and grabbed Cedric by the hair, pulling him forward and shoving the Smith's muzzle against his neck. Patience and self-restraint vanished from his body as renewed rage replaced them, quickening his heart rate and making his hand shake against the handle of the gun.

"Listen to me, you *shit*. Last week, a house burned down in Canton, Georgia. Two people died. Were your men involved?"

Cedric choked and struggled against the gun. "I don't know!"

Reed shoved the gun harder into his throat. "Like hell you don't know. *Tell me!*"

"I swear I never know what my men are hired to do! I'm just a business—"

Reed smashed the revolver against the side of Cedric's skull. "No more excuses! Do I look like I care?"

Once more, Cedric clawed at Reed's arm and tried to look away.

Reed slammed his head back against the couch and screamed into his face. "*Look at me like a man when I'm talking to you!*"

Cedric shuddered, then slowly turned his head toward Reed.

"Were your men responsible? Answer the question."

Reed had stared into a lot of eyes in the moments preceding a kill. Sometimes those eyes were a hundred yards away, viewed through a scope. Sometimes they were only photos—images of the people he was hunting. In none had he seen such total terror like the complete, consuming fear that filled Cedric's.

The shuddering fragment of a man on the floor nodded his confession.

Reed threw Cedric against the floorboards and stood up. "Do you know her name?"

Cedric just sobbed.

"I thought not. Her name was Kelly Armstrong, and she was a good woman. I don't suppose you know what that means, but it's an incredibly rare thing to find anyone good in this world. Kelly was the best of the best. Your men torched her house and burned her alive."

Reed lifted the revolver and opened the cylinder. He ejected the spent .50 caliber casings, then fed new cartridges into the weapon. Cedric gasped for air, his wide eyes fixed on the handgun.

"Do you know what they call me?" Reed snapped the cylinder shut and faced Cedric. "I know you've heard. What's my name?"

Cedric's voice warbled over the bile that boiled out of his throat. "They call you The Prosecutor."

"That's right. They call me the prosecutor—because I'm all about justice. I lay down the law, balance the scales. Or at least that's what I told myself, so I could sleep at night. But all that has changed. I'm over it, you know? I've moved on to bigger things. So you can rest assured I'm not a prosecutor, and I'm not here for justice."

Momentary hope flashed in Cedric's eyes as he peered up at Reed, his fingernails sinking into the hardwood. That hope vanished the instant Reed laid the muzzle against Cedric's forehead and cocked the hammer.

"I'm an executioner. And I'm here for revenge."

"No . . . please . . ." New sobs escaped Cedric's throat as he stared down the barrel and into Reed's cold eyes.

"Who hired you?" Reed spat out the question like a bad taste in his mouth. "Was it Enfield?"

Cedric shook his head.

"So, who was it? Give me a name, and I'll make your death quick."

"Please . . . don't kill me. I have a family."

"*So did she!*" Reed screamed and kicked Cedric in the stomach. The man fell forward, coughing and spluttering over the carpet.

"*Who are they?*"

"I don't know. I never had a name. I only dealt with Salvador."

Reed gripped the revolver, wondering if he could believe Cedric, then decided that it didn't matter. "I should kill you. You deserve to die. Do you know that?"

Cedric convulsed on the floor and didn't answer.

Reed grabbed him by the hair and screamed in his face. "I said, *do you know that?*"

Tears streamed down his face as Cedric nodded. "Yes . . . yes. I do. I deserve to die."

Reed released him and spat on the floor. "I'm glad

we're on the same page. It just so happens I'm going to let you live, because you have a job to do. Do you understand me?"

Cedric nodded emphatically. "What do you want?"

"I want them to know who's coming for them. I want them to know they rattled the wrong cage. Go back to your bosses and tell them Reed Montgomery has declared total war. Do you understand me?"

Cedric nodded again, sweat dripping off his sharp cheekbones.

Reed lowered the weapon, relaxing his finger off the trigger. He stared at the man on the floor, then walked away. Cedric gasped for air behind him, and Reed heard his hands hit the floor. A soft, metallic click echoed through the room.

In one fluid motion, Reed spun around, and the gun bucked in his hand as he pulled the trigger. The bullet smashed into Cedric's chest and sent him crashing to the floor as the pistol fell from his hands.

Reed holstered the revolver beneath his shirt and leered into the security camera on the ceiling. He lifted one hand and pointed into the lens. "I'm coming."

READY FOR MORE?

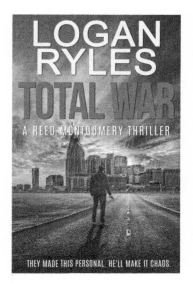

Visit LoganRyles.com for details.

ABOUT THE AUTHOR

Logan Ryles is the author of the Reed Montgomery thriller series, and the Wolfgang Pierce espionage series. You can learn more about Logan's books, sign up for email updates, and connect with him directly by visiting LoganRyles.com.

ALSO BY LOGAN RYLES

The Reed Montgomery Series

The Prosecution Force Series

The Wolfgang Pierce Series

LoganRyles.com